FREE TO VOW

FREE TO VOW

A SMALL TOWN, SLOW BURN, REDEMPTION ROMANCE

AMARYLLIS SERIES
BOOK 10

TRACEY JERALD

ALSO BY TRACEY JERALD

GAMES OF LOVE SERIES

Kickstart My Heart—Maya and Troy

King of My Heart—Amy and Brennan: Coming March!

AMARYLLIS SERIES

Free to Dream—Caleb and Cassidy

Free to Run—Keene and Alison

Free to Rejoice—Jason and Phil

Free to Breathe—Colby and Corinna

Free to Believe—Jacob and Emily

Free to Live—Joseph and Holly

Free to Dance—Marco and Lynne

Free to Wish—Finn and Jenna

Free to Protect—Brett and Jillian

Free to Reunite—Benedict and Kelsey

Free to Vow—Charlie and Rhoswen

AMARYLLIS HERITAGE

Free to Fall—Liam and Laura

Free to Judge—Declan and Kalie

MIDAS SERIES

Perfect Proposal—David and Carys

Perfect Assumption—Ward and Angela

Perfect Composition—Beckett and Paige

Perfect Order—Kane and Leanne

Perfect Satisfaction—Arek and Ursula

Perfectly Free—Brendan and Danielle

Perfect Pitch—Mitch and Austyn

Perfect Pursuit—Ethan and Fallon

DEVOTION SERIES

Ripple Effect—Cal and Libby

Flood Tide—Sam and Iris

Troubled Water—Parker and Bethany

GLACIER ADVENTURE SERIES

Return by Air—Jennings and Kara

Return by Land—Kody and Meadow

Return by Sea—Nicholas and Maris

Return by Fire—Jed and Dean

STANDALONES

Close Match—Montague and Evangeline

The Ultimate Challenge—Jonas and Trina & Julian & Elle

Go to https://www.traceyjerald.com/ for all buy links!

PERSONAL COMFORT WARNING

THIS STORY IS a standalone in the Amaryllis Series.

The Amaryllis Series may cause the reader to experience emotional triggers. In this book, the following may occur on page or be alluded to:

- Emotional trauma
- Physical trauma
- Death of a spouse (not of a main character)
- Off-page cheating/exposure of infidelity
- Marriages ending
- Sexual content

As always, to enhance your experience, please check the author's website (https://www.traceyjerald.com/) for any personal comfort triggers for the entire series.

PLAYLIST

Little Big Town, Sugarland, Jake Owen: *"Life in a Northern Town"*

Hozier: *"Someone New"*

Hootie & The Blowfish: *"For What It's Worth"*

KALEO: *"Way down We Go"*

Kygo, OneRepublic: *"Lose Somebody"*

Alessia Cara: *"Scars To Your Beautiful"*

Imagine Dragons: *"Bad Liar"*

Avril Lavigne: *"Head Above Water"*

Cyndi Lauper, Sarah McLachlan: *"Time After Time"*

The Corrs, Bono *"When The Stars Go Blue"*

Enya : *"Only Time"*

THE LEGEND OF AMARYLLIS

There are variations regarding the legend of how amaryllis flowers came to be. Generally, the tale is told like this:

Amaryllis, a shy nymph, fell deeply in love with Alteo, a shepherd with great strength and beauty, but her love was not returned. He was too obsessed with his gardens to pay much attention to her.

Amaryllis hoped to win Alteo over by giving him the one thing he wanted most, a flower so unique it had never existed in the world before. She sought advice from the oracle Delphi, and carefully followed his instructions. She dressed in white, and for thirty nights, appeared on Alteo's doorstep, piercing her heart with a golden arrow.

When Alteo finally opened his eyes to what was before him, he saw only a striking crimson flower that sprung from the blood of Amaryllis's heart.

It's not surprising the amaryllis has come to be the symbol of pride, determination, and radiant beauty. What's also not surprising is somehow, someway, we all bleed a little bit while we're falling in love.

PROLOGUE
OVER TWENTY YEARS IN THE PAST

Charlie

FOR AS LONG AS I can remember, it's been a personal mission to rescue people. First, during my time as a Navy SEAL. Now, for an exclusive investigation agency in Manhattan.

It's my job to reunite missing sons and daughters with their parents. Locate brothers who wandered off into bad choices and worse cities. Track down men and women who thought vanishing would alleviate them from the consequences they deserved to pay.

I made a career out of reuniting what had been torn apart.

So when six young adults came to me and asked me to do the opposite—to ensure they could never be found—I almost laughed.

Almost.

That is until I felt the fear emanating from them.

None of them sat at first. They hovered near the door, preparing to escape. Not a single one turned their back to me, as if they knew what it felt like to have danger rush them from behind. The one I'd later learn was the youngest clutched the strap of her camera hard enough her knuckles had gone white. The only man placed himself slightly in front of the others without realizing he was doing it.

That told me more than their words ever could.

"Mr. Henderson," he addresses me respectfully.

I gestured to the chairs. "Sit."

His voice doesn't show fear, but his pulse does. It practically leaks from his pores. "We did our research and determined you're the best."

I lean back in my chair and wait. Silence has a way of coaxing the truth out of people. Eventually, a tiny woman on the left—sable hair, eyes that remind me of the Caribbean, and an expression too desperate for a face her age—released a breath like she was about to step off a cliff.

"We need to make certain we can't be traced," she said. "None of us."

I raised an eyebrow. "That's not what I do."

"We know," a blond, with glasses says quickly. "You find people. You put families back together."

I nod. "That's the job."

Another blond–clearly athletic and if she's a day more than twenty, I'm resigning—lifts her chin. "Then maybe if we tell you, you'll understand why we can't go back."

That was the moment the room changed.

Not because of what she said—but because of how she said it. No dramatics. No plea. Just fact.

I sigh. "Start talking."

They did.

Not all at once. Not cleanly. Pieces fell out of them like shrapnel—multiple counts of child abuse, mafia hits, sex trafficking, and more. The system who should have protected the children they were supposed to be instead exploited them. Parents who sold silence. Authorities buried complaints. Systems failed spectacularly and repeatedly.

"And during that time, we only had Dee," the man I now know as Phil whispers.

The tiny woman buries her head into the shoulder of the curly haired one, who wipes her eyes. "She did her best."

"What happened to her?" I ask.

"She died a few years ago before we met Ali, Cori, and Holly," Phil gestures to the three women in the center.

He goes on to tell me about struggling for emancipation. Working while going to school. About promises made to stay together as a family. About running because staying where they were would have killed them emotionally.

I didn't take notes. I just listened.

By the time he finished, my jaw was locked so tight it hurt. I'd been in war zones. I'd seen death. But this? The six people in front of me were what was left over after cruelty and devastation had a playdate.

I made my decision. "You're asking me to erase your past. You know what that means."

Cassidy nods. "Yes, but I don't remember anything so it's different for me."

I exhaled slowly. "The rest of you? Are you certain you want to do this?"

"I do," Corinna—a curvaceous beauty with caramel-colored hair says. "It means no past. No looking back."

Holly, the camera-clutching red-head, tacks on, "No one coming after us."

The protector in me—the part that never learned how to stand down—rose up hard and fast. "You're young. Too young to carry this alone."

Phil murmurs, "We were too young to live the lives we already did."

That did it.

I stood, walked around the desk, and stopped in front of them. Six strangers. Six survivors. Six kids who'd been failed by every adult who should've known better.

"I can do what you're asking," I said. "But understand this. I won't walk away."

They exchanged glances, uncertainty and confusion flickering between them.

"I protect them. That means if someone comes looking for you, they'll have to go through me first."

Phil doesn't hesitate. "Good."

I study them for a long moment, then nod once.

Their shoulders sag collectively—not in defeat, but relief.

As they filed out later, clutching onto the fragile beginnings of safety, I returned to my chair and stared at the empty doorway.

I made a vow that day. Not out loud. But deep inside where it rewired something permanent in my chest. I would be the wall between them and the world that hurt them. I would protect them—not until it was convenient, not until they stopped needing it.

But forever.

I didn't know then how completely I would be folded into their lives, how easily the word *kids* would slip from my mouth when referring to them and feel like the truth.

I couldn't know that loving them would open the door to a kind of love capable of finishing what the rest of my life had left undone.

CHAPTER ONE
PRESENT

Rhoswen

We turn and my pulse trips over itself like it's trying to find an escape hatch. Unfortunately, the truck is moving far too fast, despite the snow crunching beneath the tires. The sound of the wind as we drive is loud in the cab, echoing the rate of my pulse as I spy a white picket fence in the distance.

This is really happening.

On Twelfth Night, no less.

A night that has been diluted to nothing more than a Shakespearean play or an evening to plan the methodical disposal of plastic tinsel. It's astounding to think it was once the second biggest night in the holiday season next to Christmas Day.

As an associate professor of history, I studied the traditions of Twelfth Night and recall reading treatises about how celebrations of this magical day involved bonfires in fields and pranksters would spill levity in their villages. While it was once called the Feast of Fools, Twelfth Night marked the end of festive celebrations before the day of Epiphany.

It's so fitting tonight is the night I'm meeting his family, I think to myself. On the night before the conclusion of the Christmas season, I would know if they blessed our relationship much like the tale of the Magi. It's also why I decided to leave my tree and decorations up until Candlemas.

I have a feeling I'm going to need all the blessings I can get.

The truck slows around a sharp turn without skidding as if he's done this a thousand times—which of course, he has. Silence, which has filled the air, for the last fifteen minutes, is broken when he asks, "Are you ready?"

My knee jiggles up and down. I glance down to the flash cards sitting in my lap. When I realized this was it—the big introduction—I spent days recalling all the names and stories he's shared over the last year. Each of his family members has their own card which is then cross referenced by different cards for the subfamilies within the village trial I'm about to willingly subject myself to.

Scrubbing my thumb back and forth across the ink I think, *If this isn't love, I don't know what is.* Outwardly, I expel my breath before I murmur, "No sweat."

He reaches over and covers my ice cold hands with his enormous one. His voice is mild when he remarks, "You're going to rub the ink off those cards."

I don't bother to look at them. "Not possible. I wrote them in Sharpie."

He hums, and just the sound relaxes something that's been coiled tight inside of me. "Right. Your favorite."

"They're in purple; not blue. So they're not quite my favorite," I blurt out.

He takes his eyes off the road for just a moment to catch my gaze. "Since when did blue become your favorite color?"

My lips curve into a helpless smile. "Since I met you. Your eyes are so shocking against the color of the sky."

He returns his eyes to the road, but lifts one my hands to his lips. Pressing a kiss to the back of it, he asks, "Is there anything I can do to help you relax? We're almost there."

Horrified, I realize we're even with the white fencing—fencing I know lines a massive farm that was restored by this truly remarkable family that accepted the man I love. I blurt out, "Quiz me. One last time."

I hear the fond exasperation in his voice, "Rhoswen."

"Please." Even I can hear the panic in my voice.

Still, he slows a little. "All right, but after this, you have to relax. They're going to love you."

"You're being optimistic."

"No, I just know them." He pauses. "Okay. Who is related to who?"

Immediately, I recite, "The main six siblings are your Freemans. In age order, they descend from Phil to Cassidy to Emily. Then there's a small gap before Alison, Corinna, and Holly who are all the same age but a few months apart." I take a deep breath. "The siblings all own and work at Amaryllis Events."

He encourages me. "Go on."

"Phil is married to Jason, a doctor. Cassidy met her husband, Caleb, when he came in to plan his brother, Ryan's, wedding. Alison is married to Cassidy's biological brother—one she didn't know she had until she was an adult. His name is Keene."

Something is grumbled about Keene. Ignoring him, I go on, "Corinna is married to Colby Hunt. Emily to Jacob Madison, who is a school teacher here in Fairfield County."

"You'll get along with him great."

Now it's my turn to mutter, "I hope so." I round out the main siblings by concluding, "Holly is married to Joseph Bianco, assistant chief of the Collyer Fire Department."

He slows down even further. "See? You'll do just fine."

"I turned the fundamentals of their lives into a final exam in seven days."

"Because you want to make a good first impression."

I hold up my pack of cards and demand, "Less sucking up and more quizzing."

"I'd like to suck..."

I shove at his shoulder. "Quiz me!"

"Okay." He thinks. "Who is most likely to offer unsolicited life advice before you take your coat off?"

"Phil," I answer immediately.

"Correct. Come to think of it, he'd give it to a stranger."

"Next?"

"Who do you not sit near during dinner unless you want your clothes ruined?"

"Emily. If she spews, I'm in the potential splash zone." I recall the stories I was told about how inevitably she laughs so hard her drink ends up on her older brother.

He praises me. "So smart." Thinking, he tries a tougher one. "Which family member has twins?"

"You mean which three. Cassidy, Alison, and Corinna all have twins of differing sex and age."

"Who will always have a camera in their hand?"

I scoff. "That's easy. Holly. She's a professional photographer."

He places the truck in Park. "Final question."

I brace.

"Who do we never let near electronics?"

A smile creases my face when I cup his cheek. "Phil because he'll screw up whatever he touches."

"You've got them all right, Rhoswen." He leans down and presses his forehead against mine. "You're ready to meet them."

My shoulders relax a fraction but that's before he adds, "I just don't know if Mitch and Austyn made it back in town. If they are, well, then this becomes a whole different thing."

My eyes dart across his face like a frightened racehorse in the starting gate. "What do you mean?" Ripping myself away, I flip through the cards at a manic speed. "I...I don't have notecards for the Kensington branch of your family. I focused on the Freemans. *You told me to focus on the Freemans!*"

I'm someone who does well when I have a chance to prepare for the inevitable. I don't know how the man next to me was a SEAL for as long as he was. Forget Hell Week; panic would have had me washing out when they asked me my name and rank. But then I realize I had a year to prepare for this. A year of quiet dinners, weekend trips. Early mornings where I woke up and found his beloved face on the pillow next to mine.

A year of him choosing me over and over in small ways that now culminate in me accepting him in a huge one.

Brushing a piece of hair off my brow, he reassures me, "Rhoswen? I haven't been a monk since my last marriage ended."

My lips press together. Even though I haven't lived the colorful life my man has, something painful needles me just below the sternum when this topic arises. "I know."

"I've never brought anyone home to meet the family."

My jaw falls open. "You haven't?"

He shakes his head decisively. "No."

"Why not?"

"Because the only person who should meet my family is family."

I absorb the gorgeous feelings his words flood me with before I blurt out, "No one's ever mattered enough that I made flash cards so I didn't humiliate myself."

He brushes his lips over mine. "Years from now, I'll be reminding you of this very moment."

I hope so, I think as he leans back into the seat. As he eases the truck back out onto the road, I reach for his hand. He squeezes it before resting it on his muscular thigh where a recent tattoo of a highland cow now rests.

A secret that's just ours.

Knowing that, my pulse returns to its regular rhythm until he turns into the drive and I spy the cropping of buildings over the vast property—the Freeman farm.

The trees act as sentinels as we pull up to a lot already filled to the brim with luxury vehicles. After the truck is parked and the engine is cut, I breathe in deep and exhale slowly like they taught me at yoga. "Okay. I've got this."

"Whatever happens in the next few hours, you're with me. You have nothing to prove."

A small smile curves my lips. "I guess it's time to see if the teacher was a good student."

He barks out a laugh before cupping his hand around the back of my head and pulling me close for a quick, but thorough, kiss. "You ready?"

"I just—I can't believe I'm here."

"I can't picture you anywhere else."

I look at him, really look at him. I study the familiar laugh lines around his bright blue eyes. The intelligence, determination, and steadfastness I've grown to lean on in the last year. The man who makes me feel braver just by being near. "Charlie—"

"What is it, my coo?"

A grin spreads across my face at his pet name for me. "We're about to step into your world and it could change everything."

His craggy face softens. "You already changed mine."

It's that little burst of love that releases me from my fears. I press my lips against his before pulling back and reaching for the door handle. "Let's do this."

I push open the door, nerves humming. I swear I feel his gaze on my back. I should have looked. If I had, I would have recognized the expression on his face—the same one he wore the very first moment he saw me.

The day everything changed for him—before I even knew his name was Charlie Henderson.

CHAPTER TWO
PRESENT

Charlie

By MIDNIGHT, it's a guarantee someone's going to ask if I'm about to get married again. For the first time since my life became entwined with the extended Freeman family, I'm not certain of the answer. After all, when you've struck out not once, not twice, but five damn times, the idea of promising "'til death do us part" feels less like romance and more like tempting fate.

But that doesn't mean I've stopped believing in love. Hell, you don't get married five times if you don't have at least a little optimism. But after number five, I stopped trusting in any kind that didn't involve the men, women, and children I consider my extended family.

After all, betrayal, the likes of which I recovered from, is difficult to forget.

I was content to remain a bachelor for the rest of my days—the badass, overprotective uncle. The benevolent great uncle. It was simpler to stand watch over the people who mattered the most than invite anyone close enough to do real damage.

There's just one thing I never factored on—meeting historian Rhoswen Campbell, when I took a trip to Scotland to see where my ancestors were from. Oh, my ancestors tried to rise from their graves when she introduced herself on the tour bus.

Then, at the site of the Massacre of Glencoe—where my ancestors were slaughtered by a branch of hers—I found myself whipping out my multi-tool to help her dig up a rock as a souvenir.

I should have known then I was a goner.

Instead of listening to the tour guide prattle on, I tuned him out. Rhoswen entranced me with details about Scotland I'd never find in history books such as which glens were rumored to be haunted, which lochs were safe to swim in—and after the tour, I'd never dip a toe in Loch Ness, and which villages treated strangers like kin—as long as you didn't botch their slang.

But what the tour wouldn't be able to tell me, that Rhoswen showed me, was how the mist along the Highlands wouldn't just become something to reminisce about as weather but a precious memory. Every time I recalled it, I'd remember the way the dew clung to the ancient walls of Stirling Castle as well as the dark waves of her hair.

I'll never forget the way she made me spew out my whisky tasting at Glenturret Distillery—which claims to be the oldest in Scotland. Granted, I had good reason after Rhoswen murmured into her own glass that, "A castle isn't considered proper unless it has confirmed sightings of at least three ghosts, two scandalous love affairs, and one sheep with a grudge from being upstaged by a "hairy coo."

Every time she drops the Scottish abbreviation for a Highland Cow with her proper New England accent, a grin tries to break free.

I knew my heart was falling over the Edinburgh Castle walls when she convinced me to try haggis, mashed potatoes, and needs—a combination of turnips and rutabaga—at Makars Mash Bar.

But it was when we arrived at the airport that I felt the immediacy of loss. I couldn't imagine never being able to follow her through a field of heather ever again. After all, it takes more than just a pretty face to have me tramp through a cemetery to discover Arria—Angel of the Nauld.

It takes someone who might be worth risking my battered heart. Still, despite being late for the post New Years get together with my extended family, I can't help but recall that pivotal moment at the Edinburgh airport. Staring into her fathomless dark eyes, I'm beyond grateful I dug down one last time for the bravery that kept me alive for years as a former SEAL.

I blurt out, "I want to see you again."

"When?" Her voice holds much the same distress as when she realized I was not willing to cause an international scandal by smuggling a cow from Scotland into the United States for her. Still, I'm touched that her anguish is worse than when she realized Clan Henderson of Glencoe is related to the long ago Clan MacDonald—the very ones her ancestors tried to eradicate.

Before I could stop it, I blurted out, "Tomorrow. Let's get lunch."

A look of sadness crosses her face. "Charlie, tomorrow we'll both be back in our respective homes."

"So, let's meet up. How about Genoa for lunch?"

"In Ridgefield?" Her brow lowers in confusion. "Wait. How do you know Ridgefield?"

"Because I live in Collyer."

"You do?" At my nod, she sputters, "But...you didn't say anything when I mentioned I'm an associate professor at UCONN who teaches at the Stamford campus."

"Go Huskies." My response is automatic considering several of my "nieces" and "great nieces" have graduated from there. I cringe inside at the insensitivity of not mentioning that either when hurt crosses her lovely face. "Hey, hey. Rhoswen, I meant to tell you."

Her eyes flick back in my direction. Her disdain aims true when she murmurs, "Was that before or after you trapped my legs to the bed and had me screaming your name?"

Fuck. I reach for her hand, but she jerks it away in a protective gesture I swear she'll never need ever again. Voice shaking, she asks, "So, what were we? Just a vacation fling?"

"No!" The word is ripped from me. "I was waiting..."

"For what?" She steps back.

I hold out my hand and admit, "There's a lot about my past I'm not able to share. Not yet anyway."

Her perfect brow quirks. "And my ancestors are rolling in their grave that I even let you spend a single night in my bed." After a long hesitation, she reaches her hand out to touch mine briefly. "Why don't we just take each day as it comes?"

The breath expels from my lungs as I confess, "I'm afraid of messing things up."

Rhoswen squeezes my fingers, bringing me back into the present and what waits beyond the massive doors. Glancing at her tucked so perfectly at my side, my heart flips over in my chest.

"Maybe walking through those doors won't be the end of us," I worry.

Rhoswen laughs, having no idea of the firing squad she's about to face. "Charlie, you love them and my educated guess is they love you just as much."

Terrified this might be the last time I get the chance to do so, I pull her into my arms and let her unique wildflower scent comfort me. Just as my heart rate starts to return to something akin to normal, I hear Keene Marshall—the man who single-handedly confirms demons exist, and somehow deserve love—snarks to his best friend, Caleb Lockwood, "And here I thought tonight was going to be dull."

"It's never dull when it's a family dinner, Keene," Caleb reminds him.

Ain't that the truth, I think. Just as I'm about to relax a bit and introduce Rhoswen, Keene opens his mouth again. He turns on his disarming smile and introduces himself. "Keene Marshall. Welcome to chaos."

Rhoswen lets out a soft laugh before accepting his hand. "Rhoswen Campbell. And thank you, but I'm used to chaos."

Caleb, the meddling bastard, can't leave well enough alone. After introducing himself, he inveigles what Rhoswen does for a living. I know, I'm certain, that by the time we reach the farm table inside, one or both of them will have run a background check on her. But before we move from the entrance, Keene decides he's not done with me. "In all the years we've known you, Charlie, you've never brought anyone to family dinner."

I shove a frustrated hand through my hair. "I thought you being a pain in the ass ended when I left the company."

Caleb snorts. "Yeah right."

Rhoswen snaps her fingers. "Oh, you two are the ones who used to be his bosses as well as his family."

Keene's face shifts slightly, not so Rhoswen notices but I do. He's transforming into the predator that, alongside Caleb, built one of the most successful investigation and protection agencies in the United States. I step forward subtly to protect my woman before demanding, "Why can't you let people be happy?"

Caleb shrugs. "It's called being protective."

Rhoswen cocks her head to the side before delivering her initial opinion. "I like it. They love you as much as you do them, Charlie."

Keene's eyes gleam, even in the twilight. "I'm glad you recognize that Rhoswen, because I have a feeling once you walk through the doors behind me, every single person inside is going to assume you are here to announce you're about to become the next Mrs. Charles Henderson."

Rhoswen blushes prettily just as the door opens and I know we're cursed because Phillip Freeman-Ross demands, "Is Charlie bringing fresh blood to sacrifice?"

Caleb, who thinks he can whisper but hasn't quite mastered the art, mutters, "No, I think he's bringing a potential wife."

Phil's agog. "One we're meeting for the first time?"

Rhoswen, as spirited as any of their spouses, drawls, "With this kind of welcoming, I wonder why?"

Both Keene and Phil laugh as they separate us to welcome her into the warmth. But as I follow along side Caleb, my lips curve.

They think I dragged some stranger into the house? Wait until they realize I've been keeping her a secret for a damn year.

CHAPTER THREE
PRESENT

Rhoswen

I'M A PROFESSOR. I studied. I made up flash cards to prepare myself to meet Charlie's adopted family by choice. All of his family he's embraced into his life since long before I knew him. I was certain I was ready.

Clearly, I was wrong.

Also, when Charlie Henderson said he had a "...few people he'd like for me to meet," he neglected to inform me it was the entire populace of Collyer, Connecticut and part of the northeastern seaboard.

Fortunately, the farm—as Charlie said the family dubbed the multi-purpose gathering space—can hold the crowd. I take a moment to admire its beauty with thick beams, pitched ceilings, as well as a Christmas tree spanning two floors. Briefly, I wonder if there are more ornaments on it than people crammed around the many tables scattered around the room before my fears resume.

"He definitely skipped a few key details when he was preparing me," I mutter to myself.

Just then, a gorgeous redhead I recognize from my flash card preparation approaches with a camera Charlie swears always hangs around her neck. She holds out a mug topped with an enormous dollop of whipped cream on top. But even without studying her, I'd likely have recognized the infamous photographer known for both her impassioned pieces and glorious wedding photos as I'm a fan of her work. She introduces herself confidently. "Hi. I'm Holly."

I hold out a hand to shake her free one. "Rhoswen Campbell."

"Can I interest you in some cider? Uncle Charlie brought some back from his trip to Scotland and when we ran out of it my sister—Corinna—spent a week in the kitchen recreating it."

My taste buds flutter in remembrance as I recall the last time I had the very cider Holly's offering. I accept it with an appreciative, "Thank you."

Her lips curve. "You're welcome."

Sipping the cider brings back a flood of memories that have been locked inside of me. After that first sip, my mouth sets them free. "Charlie and I both bought this same drink when we toured the fishing village of Fife. I wasn't sure I'd ever taste it again unless we went back." Then I realize what I said and cringe internally, uncertain if this was something Charlie intended to share.

But I'm shocked when, instead of an interrogation, Holly's lips curve. "It's you."

"What do you mean?" I try for nonchalance.

"Uncle Charlie came back from his trip to Scotland...different." She lowers her gaze, fiddling with dials on a camera I used to wonder if companies slapped on to look good. But Holly? She knows what she's doing. Lifting the camera to her face, she focuses on her subject even as she murmurs, "I see so much through a lens. Pain, sorrow, happiness. But nothing makes me more elated than when I have an up front seat to the people I love falling in love." She lowers her lens and studies my face before she says oddly, "I think the garden would be best."

Her words don't make sense but then neither does the flush blooming over my face that has nothing to do with the warm drink I've been nursing. Her lips curve into a gentle smile. "Welcome to the insanity we call life, Rhoswen. I think you'll be a beautiful addition to our daily chaos."

Before I can stammer out a reply, she squeezes my arm and retreats to the kitchen to confer with a gaggle of people I recognize not just from my studying but from the reverent way Charlie spoke of them.

"Each of them pulled themselves out of horrors most people couldn't fathom," Charlie explained. *"I'm honored they consider me to have been a pivotal part of their healing and growth and now, their family."*

As I sift through everything Charlie's shared about his family, and everything the media's plastered about them, one fear rises above making a good first impression. What if they don't think I'm worthy of the man they've always been able to rely on?

Just then, I meet and hold the ocean blue eyes of Cassidy Freeman Lockwood—CEO of Amaryllis Events—the worldwide wedding and event planning business—and the eldest niece of Charlie's found family. She's a brilliant and savvy woman who pulled her life out of the gutter to make dreams come true over and over again. Cassidy's lips curve into a warm smile, before she nudges the woman next to her.

A woman wearing the most adorable red-framed glasses that make me almost wish I hadn't got Lasik a few years ago. Curls spiraling everywhere, the blond flashes me a bright smile— almost as bright as the one she shows on the runways when her wedding dress designs are on display.

I've barely recovered from recognizing Emily Freeman-Madison when she checks a lithe blond with her hip. The woman's head whips around and her cool, assessing gaze rakes over me. In the few seconds she holds my gaze, I can tell she's already planned how she's going to interrogate me and which jury I should be tried in front of. Charlie warned me Alison Freeman-Marshall is a cool customer on the surface but has a heart so warm, it's almost been her undoing on several occasions.

Proving how well he knows his family, she tries to stealthily reach around a woman with short brown and caramel streaked hair to snag a brownie from a platter overloaded with them. The woman, Corinna Freeman Hunt, admonishes her sister without looking away from the pot she's stirring, "Not in front of the guys, Ali. It will be a riot and then I'll have to drag Brendan into the kitchen to help me bake more." But since she's been distracted, her eyes lift and by some magnetic force realizes there's someone new in the vicinity. Apologetically, she calls over, "That goes for new people as well. Sorry."

I lift my drink and smile. "I'm good, but thanks."

Corinna smiles before her brow furrows. Then she shouts, "Brendan! Get your country music ass into my kitchen. It's time to help me."

That's when my jaw falls open as country music star Brendan Blake separates himself from a different gaggle of people. He shakes his head even as he catches the apron tossed at him from the only male in the kitchen. "You have any number of volunteers. Can't I have one night off?"

"Not if you want me to keep sending you baked goods on the road," Corinna flings back.

"Fair point. Phil, get out of the way," he orders the final person in the kitchen—Phil who I met briefly outside amid Caleb and Keene's taunting of Charlie.

Phil steps out of the galley kitchen with a flourish, even as my heart starts beating erratically when he heads straight for me. Even though we "met" outside, my anxiety kicks up a notch. Charlie described him to me as, "Phil is the man I wish I could claim as my biological son. He's given up everything—and I mean everything—for his family. I wish I was half the man he was."

Considering Charlie used to be a Navy SEAL, it's hard to reconcile the jokester I met outside with the kind of man who earned that level of reverence.

Phil grins wide enough to swallow the room's noise. "We didn't get properly introduced outside. Rhoswen?" he confirms.

I place my mug down on a nearby table and hold out a hand "That's me. Assuming Charlie didn't exaggerate, you're the single person I'm most terrified to meet."

Phil barks a laugh. "I'm so sorry."

"For what?"

"You don't know us, but if Charlie exaggerated, it was in the wrong direction. He likely didn't prepare you well enough."

"For?"

Phil waves his hand back and forth. "Well, let's just say this group has no belief about family privacy. We're going to want to know all the details about how you met Charlie." He pauses significantly before a devilish smirk takes over his face. "Especially if the topic of sex comes up."

I repeat his statement as a question to make sure I understand, "You all talk about sex? As a family?"

"Well, to be fair, for a long time it was just me and the girls. They had questions and I did my best to answer them." My heart melts a little when I realize this is part of the reason Charlie admires him so much. That feeling evaporates when he opens his mouth to reassure me, "Then, it became a bonus because it annoys Keene."

I snap my eyes shut before muttering to myself, "Do not kill Charlie for failing to give you this information. You love him. He's your person despite the fact he's related to the Clan MacDonald."

Phil's delighted laugh peals out. "There's so much there to unpack and I can't wait until dinner for us to do so."

I force one eye open to find him beaming at me. Letting out a deep breath, I ask with some vulnerability, "Do you mind keeping that close? I mean, Charlie's family means everything to him and here he is introducing me to them for the first time."

Phil wraps an arm around my shoulders and tugs me away from where I'd stationed myself. "Actually, that's the kind of information that's going to endear you to them."

I meet the frosty eyes of Alison once again. Despite the fact I'm now under the cloak of her brother's arm, I still feel a chill. "Somehow I doubt that."

He's insistent. "No, really, it will." Before I can say yes or no, Phil flicks his hand to the side. "Doesn't really matter; I'm going to anyway—it's going to help me win a bet."

I choke on air. "Excuse me?"

"Holly pointed out Charlie was in love. Since then, we've had a bet on when he'd finally bring you around."

"Seriously?"

"Oh yeah." He leans in conspiratorially, despite being terrible at whispering—exactly as Charlie warned. "Cassidy had money on Thanksgiving, but the others said he'd bring you around for our annual white elephant gift exchange. Ali predicted New Year's. I said he'd chicken out until Twelfth Night." He smacks his lips. "I can taste the batch of Corinna's caramel chocolate brownies now."

I laugh—because what else can I do?—but Charlie groans behind me.

"Phil," he mutters in warning.

Phil waves him off. "Relax, old man. I'm making Rhoswen comfortable."

"Hardly that," Charlie counters.

Phil's smile widens so much, his dimples pop. "Please. Look at her. She's already handling us better than wife five ever did and we had her arrested."

Charlie chokes. I cough to cover my laugh.

"Welcome to the circus, Rhoswen. I look forward to learning more about you." He pauses before adding on, "That is if Caleb and Keene don't already have a dossier on you by dessert."

Charlie steps closer, his hand brushing my lower back like he's anchoring me to him so I don't go fleeing into the night. "Go away, Phil. The idea wasn't to terrify her."

Phil snorts. "Then you should have introduced us one at a time instead of en masse."

At this, I nod frantically because I'm certain Charlie must have left out one or two hundred people he's forgotten to brief me on. I try not to let panic take over as I try to associate the names and faces on my flash cards with the people mingling around. I blink several times as a world-famous tattooed rockstar, who has a dark haired woman perched on his knee, lifts his drink to toast a different woman. When I recognize her face, the hair raises on my arms. "Is that Kee Long?"

Phil asks, "Want to meet her and her husband? They're both close with Cass and Em."

I manage, "I think I need more sugar for this."

"You're sweet enough without any additives."

Phil snorts. "God, Charlie. Tell me you used better lines than that to win her over?"

Just then, Corinna shouts, "Soups on!"

En masse, the thousands of people who seem to multiply every time I turn my head in a different direction all descend on the long tables. Phil loops an arm through mine even as Charlie guides me to two empty chairs.

When he sits me across from the terrifying Keene and Alison, I blurt out, "No, he won me over when he dug up a rock at the place where my ancestors decimated his."

Silence descends around the table. After Charlie sits next to me on one side, Caleb on the other, I dare to look up. I never thought it would be possible but Alison's smile outshines her brothers. She reaches across the table and offers her hand. "Call me Ali. All our family does."

Keene's eyes sparkle with mirth before he turns on Charlie. "So, Charlie. Let me get one thing straight right up front."

Charlie eyes his nephew by marriage warily. "What?"

"You're in the hot seat tonight."

Out of nowhere, a roll is thrown across the table and hits Keene in the forehead. He scowls. "What was that for, Cass?"

She leans forward and offers me a quick wave, which I return. "You will not put Rhoswen on the hot seat, my dear brother. She's new."

Keene offers me a devastating smile. "I apologize if there was any confusion, Rhoswen. My sister was correct. Charlie's on the hot seat, not you."

Affronted on his behalf at the idea of his family embarrassing him, I lay my hand on top of his in a show of solidarity. "Family or not, I'm not leaving your side."

There are a few sighs around the table. Still, Keene drawls, "That's what the first five said."

The table freezes.

Charlie does too.

And just like that, I realize I've stepped straight into a past no one here fully understands—or is done bleeding from. But one thing is for certain. While Charlie may have explanations to make, the truth will still be the same at the end of the night.

Five women may have let this man go for various reasons.

I'm not going to be the sixth.

CHAPTER FOUR
PRESENT

Charlie

DESPITE LOVING every person in this room, I've come to the conclusion that outsiders should be issued battle pay as a result of dining with my family.

Rhoswen was finally starting to relax after Cassidy and Ali stepped in. She has no idea, but she's been making an incredible first impression when Keene dropped one of his sanctimonious one-liners. Not targeted at her, pissed at me.

But the bold audacity of it has her stiffening next to me. Even Ali, his wife of well over twenty years shoots daggers in his direction. Cassidy gears up as if she's preparing to murder her own brother. Someone—likely Phil—tries to kick him under the table and nails me in the shin instead.

Rhoswen tilts her head to the side as she studies Keene's face. She doesn't look hurt. She looks incensed. Which both infuriates me and sends a surge of love through my veins. It hits me in all the places I've trained myself to protect since wife number five tried to...

I level a furious stare at Keene who picks up his fork and starts eating as if he hadn't dropped a turd in the middle of our meal. Ali slaps it out of his hand, snapping, "Did you seriously just say that?"

"What? I just expressed what everyone's likely thinking." Keene defends himself.

Uneasy looks pass around the table. Keene's comment burns because he's likely right. Rhoswen squeezes my leg beneath the table, giving me her subtle strength. "I've been very close-mouthed about my past."

Keene's trademark smirk begins to make an appearance but I shut it down by jabbing my finger in his direction. "But that comment? That burns because it was said in front of the woman I'm in love with. It was completely disrespectful. What if someone had said something like that to Ali—man whore that you were?"

Keene's face transforms into a scowl while his wife and sister both hoot with laughter. Phil shouts, "You tell him, Charlie!"

Only for his husband, Jason, to murmur, "Stop being as obnoxious as Keene."

"But..." Phil sputters indignantly. This causes the usual family laughter whenever Phil and Keene are compared to one another.

To my surprise, it's Rhoswen who speaks up in Keene's defense. Her smooth as whisky voice warms my insides when she asks, "Have you ever explained your exes to them?"

"You mean the way I did to you?" I'm incredulous. At her nod, I shake my head frantically. "No! Of course not."

Like the professor she is, she tries to break down something complex into something much more basic—in this case, Keene's overprotectiveness. Compassion. "Then it's completely understandable Keene may have emotions behind whatever facts. Especially if he feels threatened in any way."

Caleb freezes from where he's been holding Cassidy back from attacking her brother. Ali blinks repeatedly as if she can't comprehend someone defending her husband. Keene lays his fork down and studies Rhoswen intently. There's a long silence before he asks her bluntly, "Were you ever in the military?"

Rhoswen tosses her head back in laughter. "No. I come from a long line of teachers, Keene. As such, my family has experienced every type of defense mechanism associated with adolescent behavior."

Despite the flush flagging his cheeks, he asks, "Where do you teach?"

"UCONN, Stamford Campus. I'm an associate professor of history who specializes in Renaissance England and Scottish history."

The second she finishes speaking, multiple voices around the room shout, "Go Huskies!"

Rhoswen immediately makes a fist with her thumb and pinky extended, like a dog, before tilting her head back and woofing in return.

Ali hits her husband. "Leave her alone. I like her."

He sighs. "Of course you would. She teaches at your alma mater."

"And Cori's, Holly's, Jenna's..." Then she pauses before flinging a smile in Emily's direction of the table. "And of course, who could forget you, Finn?"

Finn, Jenna's husband, is calmly feeding their second child—oblivious to the scene around them.

Thinking I'm saved by the bell by Rhoswen's timely intervention, I'm flabbergasted when I'm thrown under the bus by my actual nephew through marriage—Mitchell Clifton. He leans around his wife, Austyn, and asks, "You know, Charlie, the only part about your marriages I know are the ones I lived."

Keene grins at him like a hungry shark who notices chum in the water. "I forgot all about you, Clifton."

"Thanks, Keene. Makes me think my annual performance review is going to be spectacular this year."

Beckett Miller—who not only is Mitch's boss but his father-in-law—interjects, "Your annual performance review is decided by me. Not bonehead over there."

Then my great-niece Laura, here with her husband and step-daughter, pipes up. "Actually, has anyone ever heard the whole story about Uncle Charlie and his exes?"

Kalie, my other great-niece who glances at her partner—a dark somber man still getting used to the combined family chaos, muses, "I don't think so."

Jon, Laura's twin and the oldest of their generation, agrees. "I've only heard bits. Mostly the dramatic parts."

Peter, one of Corinna and Colby's sons, leans forward like the famous wolf he's grown into. "Wait, there were dramatic parts? How have I missed this?"

Lynne Bradbury-Houde, who was emotionally adopted into our clan as Jenna's best friend, drawls to no one in particular, "This is better than watching Corinna corral Brendan into cooking."

Brendan, who has been sitting with his own branch of our misshapen family tree, lifts a glass in a toast to his financial advisor. "Thanks, Lynne. Do you charge by the hour for comments like those?"

"For you, it's free," she calls back.

The room bursts into laughter. My temper rises even as the family's lost in the moment of goodnatured teasing. Finally, I boom, "Enough!"

Silence descends all around. I snap, "We're not doing this at the table."

Rhoswen leans over and rests her head on my shoulder. "It's okay. They're curious because they love you."

But it's not. Not because of the questions—hell, I'm shocked they haven't asked them long before now. They're my family—blunt, nosy, and filled with chaotic love that saved me on more than one occasion.

I just don't want anything to make Rhoswen uncomfortable and I know my family. Once I open up this door, nothing's going to be off limits. Pushing back my chair, I hold out my hand. "Come with me for a minute?"

She places her napkin by her plate before laying her hand in mine. Standing, we head for the hall. As we make our way there, my keen hearing picks up the hum of the low voices—the stage whispers that pierce the air like they're waking the dead.

"Are we finally going to hear Charlie's story?" Corinna's wonders in awe.

"Bet he won't share everything." If I don't strangle Keene by night's end, Ali should be grateful.

"I bet one of them threw something at him. He has that scar on his shoulder," Jon surmises. I shake my head. Kid's too smart for his own good. Not surprising considering who his parents are. Still, I wonder what he's going to think when he realizes it was actually a slice from a knife?

Then Mitch joins in and his calm voice settles some of the nerves inside of me. "All I know is he and my aunt are still on decent terms. What broke them up didn't ruin that."

There's so much more to it than you think. But I keep that to myself.

For now.

Instead, I shoot them all a look over my shoulder that has them freezing like raccoons caught in headlights before I lead Rhoswen back out the front door. Closing it firmly behind us with a click, I let the cool air hit my face hoping it will ease some of the tension in my chest.

It doesn't. Nothing does until she lays her hand over my heart. That's when I can let out the ragged moan I've been holding in. Without a word, she steps forward and wraps her arms around me.

I'm not certain how long we stay there, just me and the woman I'd give my life to protect. Scrubbing my head against the top of her hair, I agonize, "I should have known this would come up."

"You don't have to—"

I cut her off gently. "I do. You've studied them, but you don't know them yet. Once they have the bit between their teeth, they won't let something go. It's how we saved the girls. It's how Phil..."

Her eyes soften. Damn if that doesn't make what I'm going to share with the room both easier and harder because of who's in attendance. "So, break it down, Charlie. Your first marriage..."

"The truth is simple and straightforward." Pulling back, I pace back and forth.

Rhoswen rubs her arms up and down to ward off the chill as she waits patiently. I don't have to tell her that two and three are going to emotionally slaughter me. She already knows. Still, I remind her, "Number four is Mitch's aunt."

"You were married to her for ten years."

"He knows about why it ended—the cheating. Just not the rest of it." I shove a hand through my hair.

Her lips part, surprise flickering—but not judgment. Never judgment. "He's a grown man. With a family, Charlie. Don't you think it's time he does?"

That's when it hits me. Maybe they all deserve the whole story. Not the rumors that grew over the years. Not the family gossip, but the real version of me who fell in love. Who fell out of it. Who was too young, dumb, and too married to his job to be a good husband.

I reach for Rhoswen. "Will you stay close by?"

She nods once, steady and sure.

Thank God. If I'm going to tear open old wounds in front of the people I love, I need the woman I love beside me when I do it. Because when I do, it's going to rewrite everything this family thinks they know about me.

CHAPTER FIVE
PAST: SIX MONTHS EARLIER

Rhoswen

THE THING about this stage of a relationship is the newness hasn't worn off but the warmth of familiarity is starting to set in. I still get chills when I see Charlie's name pop up on my screen, but I know he prefers water with dinner and a small whisky after.

He teases me about my careless placement of dropping silverware in the wrong slot in the drawer. I joke with him about believing that popping frozen enchiladas into the oven is "home cooking". Over the last six months, we've built a rhythm of banter, tenderness, and respect between us.

Another plus is Charlie hasn't raised any emotional red flags, which is a lot more than I can say for some of my past relationships.

For now, it's enough.

Hootie and the Blowfish's remake of Buffalo Springfield is playing through my Bluetooth speaker when he appears behind me. One of his enormous hands curves around my hip. He spins me around before tugging me into his arms. I drop the Clorox wipe I was using as he shuffles me across the floor and into the connected living room. His body pressed against mine exudes warmth but without pressure.

Just like us, it's easy.

He murmurs, "The counter's sparkling. You're done."

I snicker, but melt when he presses a kiss to the side of my neck. A small moan escapes. Charlie must hear it because he tightens his grip on me even as his lips press against the edge of my jaw.

"Is this good?" He checks in. One of his hands grips my chin, tilting my face up to gaze into my eyes. .

I love how he does this—makes certain I'm in the same place he is before taking any liberties. Sliding my fingers up the softness of his beard, I whisper, "Perfect."

His lips lower to mine then—carefully. I tilt my head so we can fit even more perfectly against one another. I savor the way his lips slide over mine with authority. Then, when his tongue slips between my lips, the current that surges through me leaves me aching for more of him.

More of this.

I lean into him and surrender to this kiss. My hands slide down his neck to grasp his shirt for purchase. Once I have a hold, I yank him closer.

Charlie deepens the kiss, pushing me up against the back of my sofa. The growl that rumbles up from his chest sends a chill down my spine.

The heat between us isn't new, but the ache is growing with each passing day. Every time we touch, my thoughts turn to mush while my senses sharpen to the point of agony.

It's becoming harder and harder to not drag him off to my bed.

We're both gasping for breath when we break apart. I'm certain I'd be a puddle on the floor if it wasn't for the steadiness of his hands holding me upright. He murmurs my name in a deep sexy voice that twists my insides, "Rhoswen."

"Hmm?" My lips brush over the smooth skin above his beard seeking more of what I just had.

Like a bucket of ice water being tossed on me, he whispers the words no woman wants to hear at this moment in time. "I think we need to talk."

Every inch of my body freezes. There's no way Charlie doesn't notice. For a second, he clutches me against him before his hands fall away from me. Taking a step back, the loss of his warmth causes a different kind of chill. It's the kind caused by wariness because that sentence coming out of someone you care about's mouth?

Never good news.

I ease back so I can perch on the arm of the sofa. As I do, I search his face for a clue as to what's coming. He doesn't look angry or irritated, which is good. But a certain guard has shuttered down over his blue eyes. He's bracing himself.

But for what? The thought of having had this time with Charlie and knowing it might disappear causes a knot in my stomach, but I don't allow any of that to leak into my voice. "About what?"

He scrubs both of his hands over his face, as he moves around to the front of the sofa. Deciding I might as well be comfortable for this conversation, I slide off the arm and into the seat. Tucking my legs beneath me, I watch as he paces back and forth as he releases some of his agitation. He doesn't say anything, nor does he meet my eyes—both of which are their own warning.

His first words certainly don't help. "I've been avoiding this conversation. That's on me."

My heart sinks to my stomach like a lead balloon. "Avoiding what?"

He stops pacing and drags the tufted ottoman I use as a coffee table closer to where I'm sitting so he can reach out and clasp my hands. "Us. Well, not us but me."

"Why?"

"Because my past may make you...uncomfortable."

I give his hands a reassuring squeeze. "I'm comfortable with all parts of you, Charlie."

That's when he releases his grip on my hand. "No, Rhoswen. You're able to say that about the me you know, *now*. The man who knows how to be gentle. How to listen. How to talk. The one who is willing to put in the effort with a relationship to impress a pretty woman."

"You have. You do."

He leans forward and presses his finger against my lips. "Let me talk. I need to be completely transparent."

I'm certain he can feel the deep breath I take against his finger. I hold my breath for a second to steady my heartbeat. As I do, I realize, this is real.

This is serious.

Whatever he's about to share will fundamentally shift who we are to each other.

Sliding my legs off the couch so he can notch himself between them, I lean forward. "Talk to me, Charlie. What's on your mind?"

His head falls between his shoulders. "This—" he gestures between the two of us. "—isn't casual for me, my little coo."

Immediately the ice that was starting to form around my heart thaws. "It's not for me either."

His eyes shut as if the exquisite pain of hearing that is too much for this battle scarred man. Still, the tension doesn't leave him. "I'm...overjoyed to hear that."

"Then why don't you look like it?" I prod.

"Because if we both feel that way, it means I owe you something."

Immediately, I protest. "I don't need anything!"

Now, a crooked smile twists his lips. "You deserve it."

"The only thing I deserve in this relationship is the truth."

"That's what I'm trying to give you."

My mouth goes dry. "Are you saying you haven't been honest with me?"

"I have. I just haven't shared this."

"Is...is there someone else?"

His expression adopts a weary tenderness that almost breaks me. "Rhoswen, the problem isn't someone else. It's that once I tell you this, I'm terrified of losing you."

Indignant, I demand, "Why would you think you could lose me?" Then I catch the vulnerability in his expression and my tone softens, "Charlie?"

"My past is...well, a mess is putting it lightly. And before we go one step further in this relationship, you need to start understanding it."

"Charlie, we all have pasts."

He barks out a laugh. "Not like mine."

I bob my head from side to side. Knowing he's a former SEAL, I appreciate his statement. But when he takes my left hand and rubs his thumb over the base of my bare ring finger, the unsettled feeling returns. "I've been married."

I'm taken aback, not because it occurred but because it's never come up. "Oh. So have I. Post college mistake. One and done for me. You?"

He doesn't answer. Interpreting that as his answer, I surmise, "More than once."

He nods. He taps a finger against the back of my hand over and over. I think he's keeping time with the music until the song changes and his finger keeps the same tempo.

One two three four five

One-two-three-four-five

Over and over.

"Five times?" I slide back in shock. "How could this not have come up before now?" But even as I say that, I realize, "I'm being hypocritical. My own marriage hasn't exactly come up, has it?"

Charlie's expression is weary. "You tell someone you've been married, they understand. You tell them you've been married five times, they wonder what's wrong with you."

"So you kept it quiet..."

"Until I thought this might be going somewhere special."

"I can appreciate that." He turns my hand over. His fingers play with my palm as he admits, "I liked you quickly. That's not like me."

"I'm flattered."

"I'm terrified." The words burst out of him as if they've been bottled in too long.

I scoot forward until I have to use his thighs to balance or risk toppling to the floor between his legs. He wraps his arms around me before muttering, "Some of these stories I haven't spoken of in years. Some haven't been said aloud...ever."

"Ever?"

"I vowed I wouldn't scare you off." He presses a kiss to the top of my head. "But you, Rhoswen Campbell, are different. You aren't casual. You make me..."

"What?"

"Hope. Trust. Care. The most dangerous triumvirate in any man's arsenal." Before I can recognize his vulnerability, he goes on. "I need to tell you who I was so you can decide if we have a future."

I slip my hand behind the back of his neck and pull his head forward so our foreheads collide. "Charlie, no matter what you say, I'm going to still be here."

"When you know why my marriages happened and why they ended, I hope that's still the case." His voice sounds like they just announced doomsday was officially recognized as a U.S. holiday.

"I don't know the man you were, Charlie Henderson, but the man in front of me makes me feel things I've never felt before. If it took a few marriages..."

He smirks. "Few is the new five?"

I roll my eyes before exhaling and staring directly into his. "If it took them to bring the man you are into my life then maybe they needed to occur."

He swallows audibly before pressing a soft kiss to my lips. A soft, reverent kiss that brings tears to my eyes and allows him to steal what's left of my heart without a word. When we part, he murmurs, "Let me tell you everything. I'll understand if you want out."

"I won't," I reassure him.

"If you do, I'll understand," he reiterates, before muttering almost to himself. "After all, the people who lived it couldn't hack it."

"I'm not leaving."

A muscle jumps in his cheek as tension infiltrates his handsome face. "We'll see."

"I'm not one of them."

Silence falls between us. Heavy and weighted. Finally, Charlie stands. He shifts next to me on the couch. "Then, I'm going to share everything, Rhoswen."

I brace quietly, willing my voice to stay steady. "Start whenever you're ready."

The moment he does, I know there's no going back. We're stepping into a whole different level of our relationship. Charlie's choosing me through his vulnerability.

My decision, by truly listening, is to choose him right back.

CHAPTER SIX
PRESENT

Charlie

THE SECOND we step back into the dining room, the noise dies down. Expressions are smothered with guilt over what I'm sure was a steady stream of gossip. I feel no remorse because this isn't how I wanted Rhoswen to adjust to them.

But it stops now.

"Dinner first," I announce. "My past can be dissected after."

Holding the chair for Rhoswen, the rest of the meal goes as expected with curious, but respectful, getting to know you questions both for and from my woman. I'm not surprised when she forms a quick rapport with Emily's husband, Jake, and Finn, as they are both educators.

During dessert, Rhoswen is passionately pointing out the ways artificial intelligence has made teaching infinitely more intriguing and yet ridiculously more challenging in the last five years. "I have to use the very software I despise."

Curious, it's Colby who asks, "Why is that?"

She props her elbows on the table, warming to her subject. "We ask students to submit electronically so we can run their submissions through confidential AI detection software."

"Is that an automatic failure?" He's curious.

"It depends on if it's a first offense. If it is, we talk with the student, offer coaching. Maybe they had a major life event occur and panicked. If it's a repeated pattern, then yes. It can lead to dismissal. The student will fail the class and be asked to repeat it. If it's egregious, it can lead to expulsion, "

Ali's remark is thoughtful. "So, there is some type of review."

Rhoswen nods. "Also, the students may have *done* the work but the site they're citing may have been AI generated. Do we punish them for doing the right thing on the wrong site or send back the work for revision?" She looks around the table and asks, "Aren't we all works in progress?"

Corinna drawls, "I don't know about the rest of you, but we all know Phil is."

Raucous laughter floods the room. Even I'm chortling at Corinna's dig. Then I realize Rhoswen doesn't laugh. Instead, she studies Phil before pushing back from the table and making her way over to him.

Squatting down, she speaks in tones so low only he and Jason can hear, she asks him a series of questions. At first, he's resistant but Jason's lips move.

Giving affirmative answers.

But Rhoswen? I can't tell what she's thinking.

She asks Jason a question, which causes him to tilt his head in consideration. Phil's eyes widen a fraction. She turns to him again and this time her voice reaches me. "We'll talk more about it later, if you're interested."

As she gets to her feet and makes her way around the table, Jason studies Rhoswen. Once she's settled back into her seat, he nods his approval at me.

I lean over and press a kiss to her temple, before murmuring low enough to be undetected by the family. "What was that about?"

Her voice is modulated to barely a whisper. "Have you never noticed Phil's vision issue?"

I frown. "What vision issue?"

"His pupils snap to one side when he's focusing. It's a tracking issue and it may be why he has problems with complex directions."

My jaw falls open. "Seriously?"

"I have students with the same problem. I can't be sure, but I suggested he be tested."

"Well, you just won them over."

Her eyes flit up to mine. "It's just something I noticed."

"Whatever it was, it made an impression."

She smiles before resting her head beneath my chin. "That's a later issue. Right now, how are you?"

I tense up before sighing into her hair. "I think I'm ready."

Her fingers find mine and clench around them. "Then tell them your story, Charlie. They'll be just as proud of you as I am."

* * *

After helping clear up dinner, I move to stand between the enormous tree and the grand fireplace.

This is where truths are told in this home and I'm about to add mine.

For better or worse.

All these years since I first met Phil, Cassidy, Emily, Alison, Corinna, and Holly, and I'm about to lift the lid off my own simmering pot of secrets.

Bodies shift. Chairs scrape.

Conversations trail off.

One by one, every set of eyes focus on me. I can only imagine what they're thinking—this loud, loyal, impossibly beautiful family who has built me into the best version of myself. A version I never knew existed.

The version I was able to give to Rhoswen.

She's as close to me as possible—at the end of the sectional, squished up next to Cassidy, Em standing behind her, and Phil at her feet. She's about as protected as she can be without me actually being at her side.

She's trying to look composed, but after the past year of loving her, I know her tells. Her fingers twist together anxiously in her lap. Her brows are drawn together, furrowed in a deep V.

Catching her eye, I mouth *I love you.*

That causes her expression to smooth out. Her lips curve as she mouths *I love you* back at me.

The pressure in my chest releases. She has no idea that her quiet strength is giving me the final momentum to share my story.

I've made mistakes. I've taken oaths, broken them for good reason. But with Rhoswen? The vow I intend to take will be the last of its kind.

That is, if she'll have me after hearing me repeat this story.

I clear my throat, the sound echoing in the vast room. "This isn't going to be easy for me to tell. And parts of it won't be easy for many of you to remember."

The Freeman siblings exchange silent glances with one another, twisting and turning until each has met the eyes of the other five. I wait for them to give me their silent go ahead. Keene sits up as if he's prepared to jump me to stop talking.

Good. It's his big mouth that started this dumpster fire to begin with. "Also, if you have questions about anything I say, you don't ask Rhoswen; you come to me."

The room stills, including my woman. Just when she's about to protest, I lift a hand. "The pieces of my life led me to her, but the shadows belong to me."

The men I helped guide from stupidity to manhood all shoot me looks of respect. The women wear expressions of varying degrees of outrage. I expected nothing less. Exhaling slowly, I draw in warmth from the fireplace letting it remind me of the unbearable days I spent at NAB Coronado. "For years, many of you have heard rumors about the man I used to be—a Navy SEAL. That is, before I went to work for Lasky Investigations."

My namesake, Cassidy and Caleb's youngest, raises his hand. "What's Lasky Investigations?"

Jon answers before I can. "It's the company Dad and Uncle Keene bought and turned into Hudson Investigations, moron. Stop reading StellaNova and maybe..."

"Jon," my voice comes out as a sharp warning.

He ducks his head, chastised. "Right. Sorry Uncle Charlie. Sorry Chuck."

"I can't really get into my time as a SEAL except to say I blew through too many marriages when I was one."

Phil opens his mouth and drawls, "Young, dumb, and..."

"Too committed to the SEALs to be a good husband? Yes." I stop him from vocalizing the truth even though by the twinkle in his eyes, he knows he's right. Judging by the ripple of laughter in the room, so does everyone else. Once again, the room quiets as everyone settles.

They're ready for me to continue.

Dragging a hand over my jaw, I accept my mistakes in my early marriages. I just want to get through them quickly. "Let's start with the first one because if you're going to understand who I am now, you need to know who I was then." I pause, letting the weight of that settle. "Eighteen years old. Fresh uniform. Fresh ego, having just been accepted to train at Coronado. And absolutely no business making promises to anyone."

Rhoswen's breath releases softly   the only sound I notice.

Rubbing my palms together once—a nervous habit I thought I'd broken years ago—I shift my weight, grounding myself in the thick soles of my boots. "Barely old enough to rent a car. But old enough to die for my country. Too stupid to realize those two things didn't balance each other out."

A few soft snorts ripple through the room. I wag my finger at the college age kids in the room. "Don't be in such a hurry to grow up." All the college age parents howl hearing the truth in that. Their kids look outraged at my "betrayal" as I've always been the cool uncle. Instead of falling down a rabbit hole of insults, I continue.

"I met her at the beach near base. We'd known each other for maybe six weeks. I was heading out on my first deployment. She was scared. I was trying to pretend I wasn't." I huff out a humorless laugh. "And in that perfect storm of fear and hormones, we convinced ourselves that getting married would make us feel more anchored. Like nothing bad could happen if we slapped our names on the same piece of paper."

Rhoswen shifts slightly on the couch to get more comfortable. Since she's already heard the story from me, I'm not worried about her judgment. No, she's just silently offering her support. God, she always does. She's always by my side.

I could lose myself in how much I love her. Instead, I force myself to keep going.

"We were given a rare Tuesday off before we shipped out to tie up loose ends. So, we got hitched at the courthouse in downtown San Diego. She wore a dress her roommate loaned her. I wore my uniform. My team took us to In-N-Out for burgers afterward to celebrate. One of them placed a bet that we wouldn't last a year." I shake my head. "He was being generous."

Mitch, sitting next to his wife near the fireplace, winces. "Charlie..."

"I was eighteen, Mitch."

"Still."

Austyn gives him an incredulous look. "For our first date, you took me out with the intent of dumping me."

Mitch has the good grace to look abashed. "That's different."

"Only because it's the truth," she counters. "Go on, Charlie."

I wink at my rainbow haired former charge before glancing around the room at the people who have become my family over the last twenty odd years. They're all captivated by my tale, which astounds me. "The most time we spent in the same zip code during our marriage was the week after the wedding," I tell them. "I got deployed. She tried to adjust to life on base alone. Letters came late or not at all. Calls were impossible. We didn't know each other. Hell, we never really had the chance."

Laura's head rests on her husband's shoulder. "So what happened? Did you call it quits?"

"No. She did. As she should have." I draw a slow breath. "She sent the papers while I was still overseas. I signed them in a tent the size of the farm table where I was bunking with three other guys. It felt surreal, like ending a relationship I'd read about in a magazine."

"Do you know what happened to her?"

A flicker of a smile crosses my face. "I do. Once the divorce was finalized, she moved back home. Got married to her high school sweetheart. Has a daughter who opened a café not all that far from here." Quickly, I add, "I don't blame her. I hope none of you ever will."

Ali clears her throat. "I don't. I'm just trying to reconcile this with what I imagined."

"Which was?"

"That you were hurting too much to talk about it," Emily adds in.

I'm grateful for their insight. "For a while—long before I met any of you—I was. But not because the marriage ended. Because I'd made a promise I didn't have the capacity to understand. It made me question whether or not I was ready to be a SEAL."

That's when the room explodes in defense of the long ago me that none of them knew based on the man that stands before them today.

It gives me the strength to continue. Finally, knowing their bickering can go on all night, I raise my voice. "Hey!"

They immediately swallow their words and focus again on me.

"My first marriage taught me that commitment isn't a crutch for fear. That if you're going to stand next to someone, it better be because you're ready—not because you're scared."

Colby murmurs, "That's fair."

Caleb nods. "Brutal, but fair."

I clear my throat again, feeling the weight lift—just a fraction—now that the first layer has been peeled back. Not enough to breathe easy, but enough to speak the next part.

"That was number one. Number two... that's where mistakes really begin."

Rhoswen's inhale is slight, barely audible. Suddenly, I'm right back there—twenty-one years old, fresh off a deployment that stole more from me than I realized at the time.

I let my eyes drift to the fire, letting the flicker carry me into the next memory, the next confession.

"Here's where I almost never became the man I was today."

CHAPTER SEVEN

PAST: FIVE MONTHS AND THREE WEEKS EARLIER

Rhoswen

When Charlie and I first started dating, we both agreed that other than the occasional dinner it might be difficult to get together during the week. Not only did he still have his nose—unofficially—stuck in Hudson Investigations, I had classes to teach and papers to grade.

But during the week on one of our FaceTime calls, I told Charlie I wanted to plan our next date night out. On Tuesday, he was fine with it. Now that it's here, he's regretting that decision with every fiber of his being.

He looks through the windshield of my car like I've driven him through the gates of hell. "Rhoswen?"

"Yes?"

"No."

"What do you mean, 'no'?" I know exactly what he's protesting, but I want him to say it out loud. Honestly, there's a flicker of fear behind the disdain in his eyes that's hard not to smile at.

"I mean, abso-fuckin'-lutely not." He gestures at the building as if its presence offends him. "This is not the kind of date you go on after sharing your Henry VII marriage backstory."

"Should we have stayed home and watched *The Tudors?*"

"That's even less funny."

He eyes the neon sign advertising free skating until ten p.m. "Isn't this the kind of activity that's for people who still bounce?"

I lean over and let my breath whisper against his ear. "Didn't you say my tits bounced great on you not that long ago?"

His voice is thick as he remembers that very moment. "I didn't mean..."

"Uh huh."

"I mean the kind of bouncing where people could get hurt after falling."

I snort. "And not get up?"

"Hey now. I get things up just fine."

I pat his hand. "You'll be fine. You work out five days a week, Charlie."

"I'm old, my little coo."

"You'll be fine."

His eyes squint at me. "You plan on enjoying me humiliating myself."

"Absolutely." With that, I hop out of my car and jog around to his side. He lumbers out slowly, as if he can delay the inevitable. Or maybe the asphalt will somehow crack open and swallow him up before he makes it to the front entrance.

After he gets to his towering height, I offer my hand and ask sweetly, "Trust me?"

"I trust you. I do not trust the maintenance of equipment being handled by teenagers who are paid minimum wage and are too busy flirting."

I wink at him as I pull a duffle bag from the backseat. "Why not? Wasn't that you?"

His jaw drops as I drag him forward under the warm July sunshine. I've never heard a grown man complain as much as Charlie does about getting a locker, getting fitted for skates, and worst yet—waiting in line to do both. He finally tones it down when I remind him, the longer he's in line the less time he'll be on the ice. He mutters, "Maybe I can pay a few of these kids to jump ahead of us in line."

I'm hysterically laughing until he asks the attendant for size twelve skates. Then I want to swallow my tongue. *Right. That's why he feels so good...*

I'm snapped back from my fantasies about the size of Charlie's cock when he's handed men's skates that have a toe pick. Disdainfully, he holds them in between us and reminds me, "I thought I wasn't going to be humiliated."

"You'll be fine, Charlie. You shouldn't get hurt," I remind him. "Besides, this is iconic. If you had been an average eighteen-year-old, this might have been something you did on a Friday night."

"I wasn't average. Most Friday nights, I was buried in a swamp with a reed stuck in my mouth trying to breathe without being spotted. Once every few hours, I shifted over to the mud-covered sandwich they tossed into that pisshole."

I lace my custom skates and get to my feet with a flourish. "See? This is already better than that."

He stands. Wobbles. Manages to find his balance long enough to shoot me a "I'll get you back for this" look. His voice is filled with trepidation. "Debatable."

I take his hand and start to move when I realize he isn't coming with me. "Rink's this way."

"Right. Just preparing."

"We're just going to walk to the rink," I encourage him.

"Slowly, right?"

"As slow as you need to."

His breath shudders out and he mutters under his breath, "Okay. I've shot people for a living. I can handle this."

Just then, a mother with her two young children walk by us. She urges them forward with a harried smile in my direction–as if she, too, understands grown men are just children with longer legs. I don't bring them to Charlie's attention. I just reassure him, "I totally believe in you."

Inch by inch, we somehow manage to make it to the ice. He gives the kids shoving past him glares that would refreeze the ice if it were melting as they skate onto the ice like they'd been born on the North Pole. Then he places a single skate on the ice.

Deciding now's a great time for me to get onto the ice while Charlie gets his bearings, I glide out onto the ice. I do a quick spin and approach my grumbly bear. Grinning with the freedom of being back on skates, I spread my arms wide. "Relax. It's fun."

He clings to the wall as if he lets it go, it's going to explode. "It's not fun."

"Just let go and have fun, Charlie," I urge him.

The second he does, he makes a sound I've never heard from a human unless they're being attacked by a rabid raccoon. "Rhos —RHOSWEN! I can't...Make it st...Noo!" His skates slide out from beneath. He lands on his rear, with his legs sprawled in a perfect V. "This was torture devised by women to rip apart men's groin muscles."

"ACTUALLY, the ancient Scandinavians invented ice skating so they could travel over frozen lakes and waterways for hunting or to reach other villages."

Charlie's momentarily distracted by that information. I lodge my shoulder beneath his armpit and force him to glide. Mentally, I'm already calling my masseuse for a double session. The thought of that has a happy sigh escaping my lips.

"You must be a sadist if you enjoy it."

"You'd enjoy it too if you'd stop overthinking."

"I'm done with overthinking. I'm just trying to remain upright."

"You're doing amazing," I lie badly.

Charlie glances down at me. Mistake. Big one. His right foot glides but his left toe pick gets caught. His right arm windmills like he's trying to herd a bunch of wayward sheep.

It takes everything in me to prevent him from going down. With a huff, I mutter, "Double session. Deep tissue."

His hand whips around, grabbing onto my outside arm. The force almost takes us both down. Dramatically, he moans, "If I don't make it out alive, distribute my possessions wisely, coo."

"Charlie, this isn't going to kill you," I say exasperated. That's when I notice he's grinning. Actually enjoying himself. He's bitching because he's a man who hates failing at something new, not beating himself up over anything he shared with me last week.

I beam up at him before tugging his head down to kiss him with a thoroughness that has him breathless. When I let him up for air, he manages, "What's our goal with the skating? If it's to incapacitate me, you're likely ahead of schedule."

"No. You needed a lesson." I spin around in front of him and take his hands.

He scoffs. "In breaking something?"

"Preconceived notions, maybe."

He stills even more, if that's possible, considering he's moved a grand total of four feet in twenty minutes. I pull gently. "You need to learn to trust me more."

With that, his whole body relaxes. The minute it does, I push back and pull him along with me. Charlie's face lights up as the wind whips past his face while I backskate. There's times I have to let his hand go—once around a newbie with a skate trainer and a second time as we're on a collision course with teenagers unwilling to part from the next stage in their emotional courtship.

But I don't let Charlie fall.

Nor, will I.

* * *

After a short break for some hot chocolate, he wants to try it on his own. I warn him it's going to be different than if I'm holding on.

"Make sure your knees are bent and your hips are steady."

He smirks. "You of all people know how steady my hips are."

Now, I'm the one who almost trips when I recall the steady thrust of his hips into me. I bite my lip. "I remember."

His eyes sparkle. I could get lost in that twinkle that lights up the arena more than any spotlight. "I hoped you wouldn't forget."

I blush and it causes Charlie to laugh. After he's done teasing me, he announces, "Okay. I'm ready."

I glide. He stomps and wobbles.

Glide. Stomp and wobble.

It's bad. Truly awful. But the effort he's putting in makes me beam. He catches the edge of my smile and it causes him to stumble. "Are you laughing at me?"

"Never," I vow.

Something in him relaxes at that proclamation. A few more rotations and he finally—*finally!*—gets the hang of it. It's like a toddler, but he's motoring along on his own.

Then, he panics. "No! Rhoswen, I need you to—"

"You've got this. Trust yourself."

"I trust you."

Hearing him say that out loud wrecks something in me. So much that I immediately skate forward and slip my hand in his again. "Better?"

"With you? Always."

The DJ announces the final song of the night—an 80s ballad that was played at every one of my school dances. I probe gently. "So, how much did you hate this?"

"I didn't."

"What do you mean...wait. Really?"

He smiles down at me. "I actually enjoyed it." He aims us toward a wall to stop. I slow our speed down a bit more gracefully.

I open my lips to tease him, but he pulls me gently toward him, hands sliding around my waist. His voice vibrates through me when he murmurs my name. "Rhoswen."

I lean forward cautiously to capture his lips in a soft kiss.

He kisses me gently at first, careful of our shaky footing, then deeper, more certain. His hands tighten at my waist, balancing both of us. I feel the familiar pull, I've only felt with Charlie, slide through me. This kiss might have gone down as one of our top ten except it's then Charlie's center of gravity gives up being brave. One moment he's kissing me, the next his balance betrays him in a spectacular fashion.

"Rhoswen—!" His hands reach for mine. Mine try to hold him by his sweatshirt. He goes down hard. Right in front of me.

I yelp as he yanks me on top of him. Together, we end up in a tangled heap on the ice. Instead of being frustrated, he's gasping with laughter.

Meanwhile I'm frantic. "Are you okay?"

He groans dramatically. "I think my pride died five feet above me and one minute ago."

I laugh so hard I nearly roll around on the ice.

"Tell my family I fought valiantly for it."

I press a kiss to his cheek. "That you did."

After we manage to crawl off the ice, have returned his skates and are in the car on the way back to my place, Charlie's voice softens. "You know tonight turned out differently than I expected."

"How so?" I suspect I know what he's about to say but I want it to come from him.

"I thought you'd disappear after I told you everything. Thank you."

"For what?"

"For giving me a chance."

"Why wouldn't I? Did you lead a complicated life before I met you? Yes. Did it lead you to me? Also yes."

He's quiet for a long moment. Then he lays his hand on my thigh. "Then next time I pick our non-food related activities."

"Oh good," I tease. "Skydiving. Ironman training. Car bomb defusion. Totally normal."

I can hear the grin in his voice. "Keep underestimating me, coo. It's good for my ego." But then his voice softens again. "I just want nights with you. More firsts I never thought I'd have a chance at again."

My breath catches. "Me too."

His thumb strokes my inner thigh. That was the moment I realized I wasn't falling in love with this man anymore.

I've already fallen as hard as he did on the ice.

The question is, would there ever be a time he'd feel the same?

Charlie

"I CAN NAME the exact city where I stopped believing in noble intentions."

"Where was that?" I'm not surprised it's Cassidy who asks. She, too, has a city that haunts her.

I stare deep into her Caribbean blue eyes and point blank say, "I can't tell you."

Her mouth opens to object, but then it closes softly. "Okay. Can you tell us what happened?"

Caleb takes her hand and squeezes her fingers while I gather my thoughts from where they drifted to—roughly seven thousand miles away.

"People talk about war like it's noise and fire and chaos. They forget the quiet parts. The parts where you're just a man in a uniform, trying to make sense of a world that stopped making sense long before you arrived.

"I was a restless twenty-year-old convinced every person in that godforsaken place was dangerous and my assignment was a temporary inconvenience before I was shown some real action."

I lift my hands and stare at the backs of them, as if they'll give me a different answer than what I know is in my memory. "I thought I knew who I was back then. Turns out, I didn't even have an idea who I could be yet."

The memory hits sharper than the edge of a knife, and I know just how awful that feels sinking into my skin.

If hell on earth exists, we're walking through it.

We're sweeping an alley behind what used to be a butcher's market. Now, due to a Molotov cocktail being tossed through the front window, it's a smoldering skeleton of hanging hooks and collapsed wooden beams.

The air smells like smoke and fear—a stench that sinks into your mind more than your clothes. It follows you back to base, into the few minutes of sleep you manage to catch, no matter how much distance you put between yourself and it.

My XO, Walker, says, "I'm thirty and seeing this shit makes me feel fifty." He taps my shoulder, gesturing for me to watch the shadows the building hid in the left alley.

We're supposed to rendezvous with an interpreter the State arranged for us two streets over, but the splinter groups in the Middle East don't care. We're on high alert as our mission parameters change from minute to minute, heartbeat to heartbeat.

That's when I spot a silhouette stepping out of the shadows. A flash of movement.

I snap my rifle in the direction, even as I shift to protect Walker. That's when her small gasp registered along with her bruised and battered face. Her breath is labored. Panicked.

Despite the compassion that immediately wells up inside, my training takes over. I motion the muzzle of the gun directly at the center of her chest.

Hands raised, she falls to her knees in the dust. She whispers in heavily accented English, "Please, do not kill me. Please."

I take in her appearance—veil torn, ankle bleeding and twisted. Her whole body is shaking like the world was about to end.

Walker lowers his weapon a fraction. "Jesus. She's just a kid."

No, she's not a kid. Still, she's barely old enough to be considered a woman.

Returning to the room, I give my second wife a name. "Later, I'd know her as Fasa—the name she whispered when she finally trusted me with it. But in that first moment, all I saw was terror wrapped in cloth and dirt.

I lower my rifle fractionally. "What happened?"

She pointed behind her, toward the deeper alley. "Bayt...home? Family..." Her voice is raspy in the way I've heard a man's when they've been deprived of oxygen for too long. "Gone."

"All of them?" Walker lowers his gun almost to his side.

She dips her head a bit, wincing. "Dead. Blood. I run."

I blink and my focus finds Rhoswen as I return from the past. Her eyes hold the same pain my voice reflects. Right now, she's my anchor in a roomful of people who I know love me. I rasp, "Her English was broken but desperate. I was...soft."

"We need to move," Walker urges. "This could be a setup."

It should have been my first thought as well. Instead, all I can focus on is her obvious pain. I take a step closer to her. "You don't have anyone? No friends or family?"

"No."

"You're alone?" I probe just in case she didn't understand me.

Her gaze flits around, frantic. "Help me. Please."

"We can arrange for..."

She makes a grab for my gun arm and Walker's rifle snaps back into position. Her hands fly upward. With that movement, so did the sleeves of her abaya. I see the very visible abuse marks on her arms causing my fury to ignite. "Walker, lower your damn weapon!" I snap.

He does. Once it's no longer in her face, she pleads. "I help. I... know things. Heard men. Trade."

Information. Always the cleanest currency in war. I look at Walker. His eyes narrow in a "don't-be-an-idiot" look.

"What do you want?" I test her.

Her breath trembles as she voices a word I swore was out of my vocabulary. "Marriage."

I blink. "Not funny."

I jerk my chin at Walker and we start to make our way to our contact. That's when he stops cold at her fluent Arabic. It's a language I've been picking up, but still am nowhere as good as him. He whispers, "She said, 'If I marry one of you, I can leave. Escape. I can live. I have no time left.'"

"Walker, man, now you're—"

He leans forward so only I can hear him. "She saw who set fire to the butcher shop."

"The alley seemed to constrict around me. All I felt was oppression. Heat. Dust. Walker was married and we needed this to be legal to get Fasa into the U.S. There I was sucking all the oxygen from a place that had no damn air as I made a decision I didn't have the capacity to make."

Keene speaks quietly. "War makes us all fearless."

Caleb inserts, "And foolish."

"Trust me, that day, I earned a medal for being both." I drag a hand down my face. "We married two hours later."

My first marriage had more dignity than this one does, I think woodenly. It isn't a chapel or a mosque. Nor in any place that resembled grandeur or ritual. It's the back of a mobile army hospital unit carved out of a half-demolished building. Someone hung a white sheet to divide the space. One side holds the healing wounded soldiers. The side I'm on is being used to sacrifice one. The disparity is not lost on me.

The unit's Chaplin performs the ceremony. I repeat my vows stiffly, feeling the surreal weight of each word. Fasa keeps her eyes downcast until I sign the final line. Once everything was complete, she whispers, "Thank you, soldier."

"I was too stunned to realize her voice sounded more like grief than gratitude. I should've noticed that. Should've wondered why relief didn't bloom across her face. But I was fully locked in my savior complex and working out logistics."

"What kind of logistics?" Colby asked.

"To trade my marriage for the information she could give us."

"What did she do during that time?" His voice is hard, but I understand why. He's been in a similar situation as mine.

"For two days, Fasa stayed near the compound while we prepared for extraction. Kept quiet, didn't cause trouble. She watched me almost constantly with eyes that made me think I'd done something noble." I let my head fall back on my shoulders. "Looking back, I understand she was studying me. Looking for weakness. Waiting for her chance."

"To do what, Uncle Charlie?" Jon's voice rips through the air.

"So, how's married life treating you?"

"Fuck you, Walker," I growl.

It's the second night of my "newly wedded bliss," and we're stationed near the outer band of tents. We received information from Fasa, through the interpreter, that someone is going to try to steal a shipment of medical supplies from camp tonight.

I drag a hand across my forehead expecting it to come away damp, but it's dry. Reaching for my canteen, I take a drink before offering it to Waker as he downs some of the same piss warm water to quench his thirst. "Think we'll ever get used to the hot?"

"I hope not." He hands my canister back to me. Capping it off, I wish for the miracle of ice. "This is the kind of hot that makes you think you're doomed to wind up sizzling in a frying pan next to some Spam."

Snickering, he tells me, "I have to take a leak."

"Thanks for sharing. Might I suggest the quality accommodations behind our Humvee?"

"Don't want to see the size of my dick?"

"Don't want to feel bad for your wife if I do," I retort.

We both laugh as he wanders off, humming beneath his breath. Unlatching my helmet, I let my scalp breathe.

That's when I feel it.

The cold shift of air. The impending sense of death's arrival.

Only, instead of it arriving with a flash and a bang, it's a shuffle of sand. I turn just in time to catch the glint of metal in the faint moonlight that's slashing upward. Likely aiming for my throat, it slashes across my shoulder, sending raging fire down my arm instead.

Instinct drives me. I grab the wrist and snap it on intuition. A raw, feral cry escapes and I freeze for half a second before disbelief and horror twist together. My voice rasps, "Fasa?"

Tears streak her face. There's nothing of the diminutive woman I married two days ago in front of me. Instead, she screams in almost perfect English, "They have my sisters! They promise if I deliver your body, they let them live! You—must—die!"

"Fasa, let me help you," I offer, knowing what this must be doing to my new responsibility. "You don't have to—"

"I DO!" she screams. "They want SEAL. Not just an American. You."

She targeted us. Not the uniform. Not our country. Walker. Me. Not because either of us mattered but because killing me would give her a reward.

I sweep her legs out from under her and aim my gun at her. She sobs into the sand until Walker returns mere seconds later. The situation explodes into shouting, restraints, and her being carted off.

"She never looked in my direction again. Not once."

"What would you have done if she did, Uncle Charlie?" Kalie asks me.

"I don't know, to tell you the truth. Was she really a villain or a victim of her own circumstances?"

Her face is thoughtful as she weighs my words in her mind.

After a long silence, I share, "I did forgive her. She wasn't a monster. She was raised in a world where lives were bargaining chips. And she made a vow to protect someone she loved."

"Do you think she made it out?" Emily rasps.

I don't delude myself. "No. I don't. I wish I did but back then, even more so than today, betrayal was very black and white." I stare into her dark blue eyes. "But we know it isn't that clean; is it?"

"No," she whispers.

"It seeps in like poison. Changes the way you trust, the very way you love. For years, I couldn't look at anyone without wondering if they were going to try to cut me next." I glance in Rhoswen's direction and find tears dripping down her face, just like the first time I told her about Fasa.

Emily speaks up, "What happened to your marriage?"

"Technically? The paperwork was never filed. It never existed according to the U.S. military."

"But it did," Holly protests, her fingers linked with her husband's.

"Yes. And my scars from it are very real." My eyes drift over to Corinna's golden orbs. "I was given some R&R when I came home. I met up with a woman who I never really forgot."

Rhoswen lifts her fingers and dabs them beneath her eyes because she knows what's coming. That's when I fell in love for the first time and when I swore I'd never believe in God ever again.

That is until the day I met this family and they healed my heart.

CHAPTER NINE

PAST—FOUR MONTHS AND THREE WEEKS AGO

Rhoswen

CHARLIE PLANNED our next few dates. We went hiking in the Catskills. We drove to Philadelphia to see the Army–Navy game. When I mentioned to Charlie I was surprised it wasn't held at either Bear Mountain or Annapolis, he informed me that due to Philly being almost exactly between both schools, "It's the traditional location of where it's hosted. Besides, are you going to tell me you'd have turned down a chance to go to Reading Terminal Market?"

I had been in the process of shoving a Beiler's whoopee pie in my mouth at the time so I mumbled, "No," around a mouthful of rich chocolate and cream.

Now, it was my turn and we were headed north. For the last hour and fifty-two minutes, I've been pretending there wasn't a secondary reason we were driving to Boston for the night.

But there is.

Now, on our way to see the Red Sox hopefully trounce on Charlie's beloved Yankees at Fenway, I've planted a detour along the way. He just doesn't realize it yet. I held off mentioning it during his rant about drivers in Rhode Island being worse than Connecticut and my reading of the history department group chat where we were voting over which student was submitting the most ridiculous end of summer semester questions. I've read aloud our chosen winner, "'For formatting, do you prefer MLA, Chicago, or illuminated manuscript?'"

He chortles. "That's actually damn funny."

"If I was grading on sarcasm, this one would get an A. Tragically, I can't."

"Too bad."

I laugh. "The last minute panic gets more inspired every year I teach."

Charlie's mouth opens. Before he can speak, British Jane—as I've nicknamed my travel app—announces we have an upcoming exit. My humor disappears as quickly as her voice does. Instead of looking down at my phone, I slip it into the pocket of my handbag. "We're not too far now."

We've passed the sign for Worcester. The trees are lush and gorgeous. I remember when I lived here, I never thought I'd leave. There was a time when Worcester held joy everywhere I turned. I breathe in the memories without thinking and a slow exhale escapes me.

Charlie glances over in concern. "Do we need to stop?"

"No."

He tries again. "You sure? We've been in the car a while."

"Positive."

He drums his fingers lightly on the wheel, the way he does when he's trying to figure out a puzzle. Finally he gives in and asks, "What's happening inside your head?"

"Plenty."

"That's a broad answer."

"That's all you need to know for right now." I think to myself, *For about another ten minutes.*

He mutters, "Bossy," just loud enough for me to hear.

I smile despite my rising anxiety. "Don't even try to tell me you don't like it."

"Busted. I like it when you're bossy and when you're telling me you want me to..."

I slap a hand over his mouth and admonish him, "Later. You can remind me about how much I enjoy you going down on me later."

"Deal. Is there a reason we're stopping in Worcester? I mean, I can arrange for an early check in?" He asks helpfully.

"Trust me; we need to stop here first."

Charlie has no idea about the conversation we're about to have. But it's one I need to share with him. He told me about the betrayal living inside his chest due to his second so-called wife— the woman he married to save, who tried to kill him to save someone else—more than a month ago. He didn't do it for pity. He told me because he was trying to give me a choice on whether I wanted to lay claim to the complicated organ that resides beneath his Yankees t-shirt.

And just because I'm wearing a Boston Red Sox one to annoy him doesn't mean I don't want to be a permanent part of his heart. It means it's time to let him know I appreciate some of what he shared. Maybe not to the same extent, but I understand.

Because I've been betrayed too. I thought my heart was going to bleed out of my chest. It was just never caused by an actual knife. And I've never told him.

"Next exit," I pipe up suddenly.

He blinks like he missed a step. "What?"

"Next exit, please. 'Jane' is taking you a shorter way, but it can get congested."

He nods before using his signal and getting off the highway. The off-ramp leads us into a neighborhood of brownstones and narrow streets. Holy Cross is only a few minutes away and I know every turn like muscle memory.

"Left," I tell him. Then, "Straight through the roundabout." Before, "Past the one that says Do Not Enter. Everyone ignores it."

He shakes his head, muttering under his breath. "If I get ticketed—"

"You won't."

"You say that with the confidence of a criminal."

"Former student," I correct. "Completely different."

Then I tell him to park next to a fire hydrant.

"Rhoswen—"

"It's fine. Park. We won't be here long."

"There's literally a sign—"

"Charlie, trust me."

He pulls in, muttering something about how I'm going to be the reason we get towed in broad daylight but the minute he shifts into park, something in my chest tightens.

Because we're here and I can't keep avoiding the reason I

brought him here to understand. I unbuckle my seatbelt and get out of the car, my gaze locked in on the place I regained my sense of self worth.

He notices instantly something's wrong. Quickly following me out of the vehicle, Charlie's immediately protective. His voice gentles, "Rhoswen, whatever it is, you don't have to if it's—"

"I do." My voice comes out smaller than I intended. "Because when you told me about your second marriage... about what she did...it made me think of one word."

He stiffens. "What's that?"

"Betrayal."

He doesn't speak. He just waits knowing there's more I'm about to share.

I point at an old brick building across the street. "The paint is fresh instead of the way it's always peeling in my memory. I have no idea if the second-floor balcony is permanently crooked from the parties we threw. The bay window was my bedroom. It used to have cracked glass in one corner."

"This was your apartment?"

"Senior year," I add. "Holy Cross. I lived there with another girl. We had one bathroom, a mouse we refused to name because we were determined to eradicate it, and a fire alarm that went off whenever someone toasted bread on any setting above four."

A faint smile touches his lips. Good. I need the softness for what's coming next.

"Before that, I lived off campus with my husband." I feel Charlie stiffen next to me. I force myself to remain calm as I continue. "We'd dated since I was a freshman. Got engaged in the summer between our sophomore and junior years. Married just before senior year. It felt like...everything."

Charlie's smile disappears. His brows pull down. He reaches for me, but I sidestep him. I can't have him hold me while I tell this story. My voice takes on a distant note. "I had a work-study job as a TA. He'd pick me up in our beat up car when it was late at night. Sometimes, we'd sit on the couch and imagine what our future would look like. Hell, there'd be times we'd pick out names for our future kids even though we weren't planning on having any for like seven or eight years."

Charlie's jaw works, but he says nothing.

"One night," I continue, "I came home early. I must have caught something from one of the students. I tried to suck it up until the projectile vomiting started. I called a cab. The ride home was hell."

"I know that feeling. The kind of bug where your bones hurt and your skin feels like it's humming?"

"Exactly." I swallow. "I never thought I could feel that awful until I walked into our apartment. That's when I heard the sounds coming from our bedroom."

Charlie sucks in a breath. "Who?"

"I was just in time to see him get off with my former roommate."

"Your former roommate?"

I nod.

"He did that in *your* bed?"

"Yes."

"And she—"

"Didn't even bother to get up," I say. "Just pulled *my* blanket over her tits and said, 'We didn't expect you back yet.' Like I was the intruder."

The air shifts. He's not breathing normally anymore. Then again, neither am I.

His voice is barely more than a growl. "What happened to them?"

"They built a life together," I say simply. "Got married a year later. Bought a house somewhere outside Providence. Last I knew, they had a dog."

He's incredulous. "You still follow them?"

I'm quick to correct him, "No! I haven't seen them since the day I demanded my half of the deposit back and moved here. But social media has a way of making ghosts try to friend you every few years."

"Why did you bring me here? Why not to your old place with him?"

"Her former roommate told the bitch to pack her shit and move out." I jerk my chin to my former apartment. "So, I moved in. This is where I lived while I dismantled my marriage and finished college."

Anger, sympathy, regret chase each other across his face. "Rhoswen..."

I interrupt whatever he's about to say. "I'm telling you this because when you told me about your past, you looked at me like you were waiting for the part where I'd decide you were too much."

He doesn't deny it.

"I may not have been through what you have, but I do understand what it means to have your heart broken, to have your sense of trust destroyed. I know betrayal. Not like 'hold a knife and try to kill me' betrayal. But I know what it feels like to have your entire understanding of the world change in an instant. To wonder if you will ever believe in anyone ever again."

His bright eyes are filled with pain and soft with emotion—just for me. "You didn't deserve that."

"No," I agree. "Then again, neither did you." I reach for his hand and hold it to my cheek. "I hate you went through your pain alone."

He murmurs, "I hate you went through what you did, but I'm not going to lie. If you hadn't, you wouldn't be standing here with me. And that? I'm grateful for."

The summer air simmers between us. Somehow, I know, making myself vulnerable to Charlie was the right move. I can feel another thread binding our hearts together.

"Rhoswen," he says quietly, "Do you know what the first thought that went through my mind was after you shared your story with me?"

"What?"

"One day, when I introduce you to my family, I'm going to be proud to have you on my arm."

Tears well up in my eyes. "Charlie—"

He rubs his thumb over the apple of my cheek. "We're building something strong. Something honest. Something I've never had before and I want it with you, my little coo."

A tear trickles out of the corner of my eye. He swipes it away. My breath shakes. "Is that a promise?" I ask softly.

"No."

He pulls back just enough to look me in the eyes. "It's a vow."

And for the first time in a very long time, I believe a man when I hear that word used on this street.

CHAPTER TEN
PRESENT

Rhoswen

CHARLIE CLEARS his throat before continuing the story. I know what's coming even before he braces his hands on his thighs. The defeated posture speaks volumes. His head suddenly swivels toward me. When our eyes meet, I pucker my lips and blow him a kiss.

His tension ebbs, as he draws strength from the gesture. I don't lose eye contact with him, even when I lift my hand from my lap and swipe away my tears. Charlie knows how I feel about the tragedy of his third marriage.

In my opinion, it's the only one that counts. It's the one he entered into with his full heart.

And it shattered his heart, making him into the man who stands before us all at this moment.

My love for Charlie didn't begin today. But now, the rest of them get to see how their lives would be impacted by his third marriage.

"Until Rhoswen, I never thought I'd speak of my third wife ever again unless it was during a clearance investigation."

This causes every male who Charlie's ever worked with in the room to sit with a little more awareness. It occurs with a scrape of a chair, a glass being placed on a table too hard. Little movements that show he has their full attention.

As I knew it would be when he finally came around to speaking about Mara, my sole purpose is to provide Charlie with as much strength as I can. From my own heart being shattered, albeit in a completely incomparable way, I know presence can be its own form of devotion.

That's what he needs right now.

He draws in a slow breath before speaking, "I met her again at our ten-year high school reunion. Her name was Mara Flores."

There's a subtle reaction to the name—a softening before everyone stiffens at the past tense. "Was" seems to echo around the room bringing a darkness I'm certain few in the room are prepared for.

"We grew up two houses apart," he reminisces. "Same schools, same teachers. Same summers at the pond that felt endless when we were kids. She was my first kiss, my first love. Not dramatic. Fond. The memories you pull out when you're lying in a desert wondering about people from home. That's the relationship I had with Mara."

His voice is calm, but something under it warns the room there's worse to come.

If only they knew what I do, I think. Maybe they'd have stuck to the jesting and cheer of Twelfth Night instead of forcing Charlie's Epiphany.

His smile is just as bittersweet as when he told me the story six months ago. "When I left to join the Navy, I wasn't leaving her. I was just doing what I planned from the time I was a kid—I was going to become a SEAL."

Someone exhales softly. He goes on, "We lost touch when I joined the teams. Life happened. She stayed. I left. Ten years passed."

His gaze turns inward. "After the Middle East, I went home. I needed some R&R. Walker was sent back to his wife. The two of us had six months to get our heads on straight. My mother—God rest her soul—had this idea of feeding me with enough fried chicken and apple pie to make me resign my commission. When that didn't work she said I should go to my ten year class reunion. Reconnect with some friends."

I allow myself a slow blink because here's where Charlie's story becomes both beautiful and heartbreaking.

"When I walked into that reunion, I wasn't expecting anything from anyone."

"What happened?" That question comes from Kee Long. Her husband Benedict squeezes her shoulder.

"Mara was there. Older, but still Mara. She had this innate talent for taking one look at me and knowing I was lying about being okay."

A faint smile ghosts his mouth. I know it won't last for long. "We left the reunion. Walked to the lake. Talked until sun up. Caught up on a decade in what felt like minutes. Things I would have had to have explained to other people? I just had to look at Mara." He blinks his eyes rapidly. "She was so much like the female version of me, I felt like I regained a part of myself I didn't know was missing."

His fingers flex once at his side. "We were engaged two months later." No one challenges it. The people in this room know this wasn't impulse; it was inevitability.

"She wanted a big wedding." Charlie's lost in his memories. "It was the kind you only do once—the kind if we'd have had the money, we'd have paid someone like Cassidy to plan. It was so important to both of us that it was done right."

Cassidy, honored by Charlie's words, scrubs her face against my shoulder to wipe away her tears.

He keeps on going. "The whole town was invited—family, neighbors, teachers. Seemed like everyone who was there remembered us when we were just kids and had a story that ended with 'We always knew you'd end up together.'"

He swallows. "She was a vision in her white lace gown. Me? I wore my dress blues." Something in his voice must alert them because the tension in the room ratchets up. I can feel it. Cassidy's hand reaches for mine. That's when Charlie exhales. "That was the second to last time I ever wore them."

I hear a voice murmur, "I have a bad feeling..." I don't take my eyes from Charlie to suss it out.

But they're right.

Instead, I take shallow breaths so I can support Charlie better than I did the first time I heard about Mara.

May God rest her soul.

"We returned to San Diego after my R&R. I passed all my psych evals. They deployed me back with the team three months later. Routine assignment. But nothing that raised alarms. I knew I'd be out of the country for a while, but we talked when we could. Letters when calls weren't possible."

He pauses.

"She always ended the same way. 'Come home to me. I love you.' I always promised I would and told her I loved her, too."

Charlie bends over at the waist. A softer version of the inhumane sound he made when he told me about Mara pierces the air. He grates out, "Three months into that assignment, she was abducted."

The darkness that has lived in Charlie for so long has now shattered like a glass bottle hitting a hard floor. Everyone's affected. Tears fall freely from my eyes now that his wound has been lanced. Cassidy's squeezing my fingers so hard in her agony, I'm certain there's going to be swelling. Someone across the room sniffles. Someone else mutters something vicious under their breath.

We're all united under a single source of pain—Charlie's.

"What happened?" Keene grits out.

"She was a pharmacy tech. Left work late. Witnesses saw two men force her into a van. Broad daylight. No explanation. No demands." Charlie's hands curl into fists slowly, deliberately. "There was no ransom. No political message. No leverage. She wasn't taken because of me. She was taken because there are people in this world who hunt for vulnerability."

I feel that word—*hunt*—settle heavily.

"But I didn't know," he continues. "Our unit was dark. No communications. For forty-eight hours, my wife was missing and I had no idea."

Cassidy rips her hand away to press it to her mouth. Someone is openly sobbing now.

"When we came back online, my commanding officer handed me a satellite phone," Charlie's voice is monotone. "It was my mother."

He swallows repeatedly before he pushes out, "They'd found her body. Autopsy shows she was killed the first night," he says quietly. "Before anyone traced the vehicle. Before anyone could help her."

No one speaks. No one moves. Even grief seems uncertain where to fall, the room is so fractured. Charlie's chest lifts on a breath that doesn't fully release.

"They flew me home and all I remember was getting dressed into the same uniform I put on for her to walk down the aisle of a church to me just months earlier. No one knew what to do with their grief." He stares at the floor. "I buried her and when I did, I buried the man I was with her."

The truth of that statement sits heavy and absolute. Cassidy reaches over to offer me comfort but I don't need it. Mara's Charlie did die that day.

The Charlie who loves me rose from scattered ashes. He's a whole different man and it's due to the people in this room. But I don't say that.

Not yet.

"I left the teams after that," he says. "Not because I stopped believing in the mission. But because I couldn't live with leaving anyone behind without at least *trying* to find them. Not ever again."

He lifts his head then, eyes scanning his family slowly.

"For a long time, I thought that was it. That I'd just wait to die. That the pain of a loss this great was something you endured until your number came up. But something happened."

"What's that, Uncle Charlie?" Jon asks.

"I couldn't stop seeing her face in every missing poster. Every Amber Alert. Every case buried in the back pages of a newspaper. I couldn't unsee how fast someone could vanish. How thin the time was between here and gone."

I know what's coming and a swell of pride surges through me. *He could have laid down and given up, but he didn't. As a result, he saved all of you,* I think to myself.

"So I started helping," he continues. "Unofficially at first. Tracking leads. Sitting in rooms with families who were waiting for news that might never come."

His voice steadies—not because it hurts less, but because inside his pain, he's found purpose. "I realized I was never going to stop loving Mara just because she died. Just like people will never stop loving their loved ones who went missing. Time doesn't close those kinds of wounds. All it teaches you is how to cauterize it enough to function."

Someone—Keene, I think—mutters, "This is how I felt all those years." Aside from that, the room is silent, rapt.

"So I made it my job to keep looking. To be the one person who doesn't tell them to move on." His eyes lock on the men married to the Freeman women, before they swerve to Phil. "That's why I was in the right place at the right time to be there for the six of you."

No one speaks for a long moment. Charlie's drained. The room is permanently altered, just the way I was. They knew he was strong, but even I'm not certain if they knew how strong he was.

Until now.

I stand. Slowly. Deliberately.

His gaze flickers in my direction, unwavering until I stand in front of him. I don't touch him. I wait, because the next move is his.

He exhales, just once before he reaches for me. Just a brush of our fingertips. When our palms meet, his shoulders drop—not in defeat but in relief. I've known for six months and I can't imagine how he's been carrying this for decades.

Tonight, he finally set it down.

Let others embrace his pain as he did theirs.

As I let him draw whatever energy he needs to go on, I know one thing with certainty. This man doesn't love lightly. He doesn't love halfway. He doesn't love without cost.

Knowing what I do, I'm blessed he loves me.

CHAPTER ELEVEN
TWO MONTHS AGO

Rhoswen

Tide Pool is the kind of dive bar that makes you feel like you're being let in on a secret. There's no neon sign buzzing. The floor is quite possibly smoother than the hardwoods in my small cottage in Chester. Before we got there, Charlie warned me, "I've never not been here and stopped a fight."

"Then I can't wait to see what the night brings."

He huffs, as if that's a deterrent.

The place is crowded but not packed, but the second Charlie steps through the doorway, I'm not sure if it's because the bartender called attention to him with her proclaiming, "Well, look who the cat dragged in!" Or if it's because his dark jeans, boots, and henley—not to mention silver fox scruff—makes me want to drag him out for some one on one time instead.

He rolls his eyes at the bartender before guiding me toward the empty stools she jerks her chin at. "You sure you're okay with this place?"

"I'm positive," I say. "I can't say I've been to a dive bar unless we actually stay for a while. Plus, I think half the population is side-eyeing either you, me, or want your boots."

He glances down, amused. "They are good boots."

"They scream recently spit shined."

"Impossible. They're made of waterproof hard tactical nylon."

"I understood two of those words, yet they still scream expensive."

A low laugh rumbles out of him that makes me smile just by being close enough to hear it.

We take the stools at the bar. Charlie automatically chooses the one with the best view of the room—habit. The bartender who recognized him slides over with a towel slung on her shoulder and a cautionary expression that says she's ready for whatever comes next.

"Charlie," she says. "Tell me it's just you and not the rest of the looney bin tonight."

"You lucked out, Jess," he replies.

"For the moment." Her eyes flick to me. Assessing. "You're new."

"I am."

Charlie's hand settles at the small of my back—casual to anyone watching, but I know what it is—a claim.

The bartender's gaze softens by a fraction. "What're you drinking?"

Charlie's response is immediate, "Whatever is on tap."

I say, "Tequila. Top shelf."

Charlie's winces. "Professor."

"What?" I blink. "What's wrong with tequila?"

"Nothing good happens at this bar when someone associated with my family drinks tequila."

"Are we related?" I throw back at him.

Jess smirks. "I like her."

Charlie's mouth twitches like he wants to argue but doesn't. "Fine," he says. "But if this goes to hell, I'm holding you responsible."

I'm a grown woman. I snort. "Whatever."

He makes a sound that's a cross between a growl and a laugh.

Even as Jess pours, my eyes sweep the room. Stage with an impressive stack of amps. Pool table and dart boards in another room. Outside, I can spy a deck and wonder where it leads to. The customers lend to the atmosphere perfectly. There are guys who look like they've been coming here since the invention of alcohol and a group of women in sparkly sashes giggling too loud.

It's the kind of night where anything might happen and nothing will be remembered correctly unless someone's taking a video. Once Jess delivers our drinks, I proclaim, "It's perfect."

Charlie lifts his beer, keeping his body angled toward me. His thigh brushes mine under the bar. "How's your week been?" His eyes are steady, but the question isn't casual. It's an opening. A check-in. A quiet way of asking if I'm still okay with us. Him.

"Better now," I say.

His gaze drifts over my face, lingering on my mouth like it's a problem he'd like to solve. He watches me for a beat. Then he nods once. Accepting.

"Okay," he says. "Then what are your plans for after that tequila tonight?"

I swirl my drink. "A desire to watch you lose control."

He huffs. "Are you propositioning me?"

"Charlie." I let the word drip with disbelief. "You're a menace."

His smile flashes—quick, bright, gone too soon—but it does something to me anyway. I can feel my body respond, heat gathering low and slow. We trade quips and are halfway through our first drinks when I feel him tense up.

That's when something different crawls up the back of my neck. Glancing over my shoulder, a man a few stools down watches me with the kind of arrogance that makes my skin itch. Mid-forties and rotund, if I'm being generous. Red-faced. A little too comfortable in his beer sweats. He lifts his glass in a lazy salute.

I whip around to face Charlie. His expression doesn't change, but his posture does. The air around him tightens, like a warning.

"Don't let someone like that ruin our evening."

"I wasn't going to start anything," he says mildly.

"You were absolutely going to do something."

"I'm merely observing."

"Mm-hmm."

But of course the man can't do simple and stay away. No. Instead he shoves away from the bar, grabs his beer, spilling half of it down the front of his shirt. Charlie murmurs, "Incoming."

"Of course." The second he's next to us, he squints one eye at me, not even bothering to acknowledge Charlie's presence.

Big mistake.

"Hey," he says, voice slurred with too many beers. "I'm wanna make your night interesting."

Charlie's hand lands on my thigh to let me know he's there if I need him. I smile politely. "My night's already interesting with the man I'm with. Thanks, but no thanks."

The man laughs, like I've said something cute. "Nah, sweetheart, I mean *interesting*. I haven't wanted to jack off to curves like yours since—"

I tune him out as Charlie shifts. Not anything dramatic, like chairs falling down, but enough I know he isn't going to let this go on for more than another minute. I open my mouth to tell this guy to beat it when the guy's eyes flick to Charlie and back to me before making the mistake of dismissing Charlie again.

"And what I could do from behind," I catch him droning on. Unfortunately, he leans closer making me want to pinch my nose shut at the sour smell of sweat and beer. "Holding onto that mane of yours? Fuck, yeah. You'd forget your own name."

My cheeks heat—not from embarrassment, but from the sheer audacity of this buffoon. The statement is obscene.

I set my tequila down. Turning my head, I look the man dead in the eye. "Go away."

He grins, expelling more of his noxious breath. "Come on. Don't pretend you don't want that."

"I don't," I say flatly. "And you're standing too close."

His grin falters, then returns sharper. "You got a mouth on you. I can put that to work too."

Charlie's voice is lethal when he addresses this loser. "Step back."

The man aims a thumb in Charlie's direction, even as he falls off balance. "Who's the silver-haired dude? Your big brother? No, wait. Your dad?"

Charlie's smile is razor-thin. "Neither."

I feel the shift in my man—the restrained edge of fury as he decides how much force will be necessary to protect me.

The man leans closer—idiot. "I'm just saying, if you want a real man—"

Charlie moves so smoothly it's graceful. One moment he's seated, the next he's upright, blocking the man's access to me with his body. He makes the other man shrink to being inconsequential with one single move.

"You get one warning," he says quietly. "Then you're going to have a very bad night."

The man's grin wobbles. He glances around like he expects backup.

No one steps forward. Because at Tide Pool, people know Charlie and no one wants to be on his bad side. I slide off my stool and step around Charlie—not to stop him, but to reclaim my own space. I look the guy in the face again.

"Go," I say. "Before you embarrass yourself more."

For a second, the man's pride fights his survival instinct. Then he scoffs like he's choosing to leave, not being forced.

"Whatever," he mutters. "You'll regret a good time."

He walks off, shoulders stiff, pride in tatters.

The moment he's gone, Charlie exhales—controlled, contained. I touch Charlie's forearm lightly. "Hey."

His gaze drops to me. It's dark. Not angry. It's burning with an intensity that kicks up my pulse a notch. I step closer, sliding my hand up his chest, feeling his heartbeat under my palm. Fast. Steady. Controlled.

I lick my lips without thinking.

His eyes track the movement. His jaw tightens.

I feel the moment shift—the bar noise returning, laughter rising around us, but between us, everything sharpens. I lean in, close enough that only he can hear. "You know," I say softly, "I really don't need to finish my drink."

He drops his head slightly, his mouth near my ear. "Rhoswen."

The way he says my name is not a warning, it's a promise.

I pull back just enough to see his eyes. "Tell me what you're thinking."

His gaze dips to my mouth again. "I'm thinking I don't like anyone looking at you like that."

"I don't like it either," I say. "But I liked watching you decide I was worth standing up for."

His breath catches—subtle, but there. "Careful. You're giving me ideas."

I tilt my head back, my smile turning wicked. "Good thing I'm already having them."

His hand slides firmly around my waist. "We should go."

Heat coils through me. My pulse thunders. "Then take me home."

"Bye Jess."

"See ya, Charlie."

He tosses a bill on the bar without looking, guides me out with a hand at my back, shielding me from the crowd—not possessive, exactly, but deliberate.

Outside, the cold hits my cheeks, and I laugh—one sharp, breathless sound. His gaze drops to my mouth. "Get in the car," he says, voice rough.

"Yes, sir," I tease.

His eyes flare.

As we head into the night, I know exactly what comes next. And it has everything to do with the way Charlie's looking at me right now. He's no longer restrained.

His hunger is taking over.

And nights like this always end up exceptional for me.

CHAPTER TWELVE
TWO MONTHS AGO

Rhoswen

WE PULL into his driveway faster than usual. He cuts the engine, but neither of us moves immediately. The porch light casts a soft glow across his profile, highlighting the tension in his jaw, the controlled rise and fall of his chest.

I reach out, resting my hand on his forearm. "Charlie."

He turns toward me, and whatever he's been holding onto snaps. His hand comes up to cup my jaw, thumb brushing the corner of my mouth. I lean into the touch, ready for whatever, when he murmurs. "Inside. Now."

I nod, breath already shallow. We don't rush, but there's urgency in every movement as we climb the steps, unlock the door, step into the quiet warmth of his house. The door closes behind us with a soft click. That sound frees me—sealing us in our own cocoon.

To my surprise, Charlie doesn't kiss me right away. Instead, he stands there, hands balled at his sides, searching my face like he's astounded by the choice I've already made. I close the space between us until my body is nearly flush with his. Tilting my head, I meet his gaze head-on.

That's all it takes.

His mouth finds mine with a hunger that steals my breath—not rough but thorough. Like he's been imagining this moment and denying himself for far too long. His hands slide to my waist, anchoring me, pulling me closer until I can feel the hardness of him everywhere.

I grip the front of his shirt tight, grounding myself in the reality of him.

He kisses me deeper, slower now, like he's savoring, like he's memorizing the way I respond to him.

When he breaks away, his forehead rests against mine. "Rhoswen," he murmurs, voice rough. His thumb brushes under my chin, lifting my face slightly. His gaze softens—just for a second—before the heat returns. "I won't tolerate anybody disrespecting you."

My heart tightens. "That's why you got so angry."

"Yes." His eyes hold mine. "He spoke to you with contempt. That was unacceptable. You deserve the world."

The care in his words sends a rush of warmth through me. My pulse stutters. "Kiss me, Charlie."

He kisses me again, slower this time, his hands tracing my back, learning the shape of me like this is something sacred. The kiss deepens, heat blooming everywhere he touches, but there's restraint there too—intentional, deliberate.

I tug lightly at his shirt, breaking the kiss just long enough to murmur, "You're still holding back."

His mouth curves faintly. "Habit."

"I don't want you to," I say.

He studies my face, searching for hesitation. He doesn't find it. Instead, he spins us to back me gently against the wall, one hand braced beside my head, the other still at my waist. His body shields mine completely, not trapping me, just... surrounding.

"You still good?" he asks, voice low.

"Yes," I breathe. "Very."

His mouth trails along my jaw, down my neck, unhurried. Every touch feels intentional, grounding, like he's reminding himself—

and me—that this is real. That we're choosing each other in this moment, not reacting to anything else.

"I don't take this lightly," he says against my skin. "I will never treat you like you mean less than everything."

"I know," I whisper, fingers threading into his hair. "That's why I fell in love with you."

The words hit him hard. I feel it in the way his breath stutters, in the way his grip tightens briefly before easing again. He lifts his head, eyes locked on mine. "Say it again."

I cup his cheeks. "I love you, Charlie Henderson."

His forehead leans against mine, terror temporarily overriding lust. "I can't lose you too."

My chest warms, something deep and steady settling there. "I'm not going anywhere," I vow.

"Come with me," he murmurs.

He takes my hand, leading me down the hall, the house is dim and quiet around us. The door to his bedroom closes softly behind us, and the world narrows to the two of us—steady, certain, chosen. His mouth claims mine again, and this time there's no holding back—only connection, only heat, only the slow unraveling of everything we've both been bracing against. When he finally pulls away, his forehead rests against mine, breath warm, voice hushed.

I know exactly what's coming next. Charlie and I have physically connected numerous times since we started dating.

He hauls me to him so I'm on the very tippy toes of my feet. He touches his lips against my forehead, then down each cheek. My nose, my chin. Then, gently over my lips. Each brush causes the blood to beat faster in my veins.

Lips parting, I moan, "Charlie, kiss me."

He does. At first, it's like fire flickering. Then, I wrench my mouth from his. "Too many clothes."

"Right," he mutters. With one arm, he rips off his henley showing off his toned body that still sports a six-pack.

My mouth waters even as I wrench my sweater over my head. I'm too distracted by the feeling of his skin on mine.

He drags his mouth down the side of my neck leaving a chill in their wake.

Charlie fumbles with the clasp of my bra. Shortly after, that's been discarded on the floor, he's spinning me around so fast I feel like I'm falling.

No, I am actually falling. I land in the middle of his enormous bed leaving his hands free to roam over my bare skin. His fingertips graze over my shoulders, down my arms, even over my fingertips before making their way up the center of my torso so they cup my breasts.

At that point, I slide my fingers into his close cropped hair and pull his head toward my bare chest. He takes the prompting with no resistance. His lips close over a turgid nipple where he begins a slow suck intermingled with languid strokes of his tongue.

I writhe, his every movement sparking the kind of fire I've never experienced with a lover before. One I know I'll never experience again in my life.

After all, real love is the difference between good sex and the kind that burns the world down. With Charlie, all he has to do is hold my hand and I feel like there's kindling catching. With what he's doing to my body right now, I'm already primed for a three alarm blaze.

Charlie stands and yanks off my ankle boots and leggings, taking my panties with them. Now, I'm laid out before him—stretch marks and all. But with him, I don't care. He makes me feel like I was created for his hands, his mind.

His heart.

He nuzzles the space where the organ that beats just for him rests between my breasts even as I move my hands to the waistband of his jeans where I fumble with the heavy belt buckle. Standing to his full height, he makes quick work of it.

The lowering of his zipper causes goose bumps to rise up on my skin. I open my arms in welcome and he falls into them. "I can take my boots off," he offers.

"I don't want to wait that long." And it's the truth. I'm in such a hurry to have him become one with me, I don't care if he's barefoot or wearing bunny slippers. I need to feel him connected to me.

I want to hear Charlie tell me he loves me while his body is sliding in and out of mine.

As if he can hear my thoughts, he reaches down and drags the head of his cock up and over my clit before dragging it back down to my entrance. Over and over, taunting, teasing. Getting himself wet, getting me drenched. Fortunately, I'm on the shot to regulate my hormones and we're each tested regularly, so we've dispensed with protection.

Soon, it will be him and his long cock sliding into me. Panting, I beg, "Please," hoping this speeds him up. There are some nights he'll hold me on the edge for hours.

"I want to hear you say it again," Charlie braces himself on one arm above me. The other holds his cock away. Then he stills before notching the head against me. "No, I *need* to hear you say it."

Wrapping my thighs around his hips, I reach one hand up and grip his wrist that's planted near my head. My other hand, I use to cup his jaw. "I love you, Charlie."

His lips tremble before he pushes himself forward. Once he's bottomed out, he leans down and holds himself firmly lodged inside of me. He takes my lips in a searing kiss. The second our lips break apart, he murmurs, "I love you, Rhoswen."

His shaft moves in and out as his hips roll slowly. Each time he repeats the motion, I arch into him—intuitively doing what women have done for all of history.

Beg their men for more.

For all of them.

I need the beads of his sweat on my skin.

I score his back with my nails.

And over and over, I keep reminding Charlie of my love. My devotion. Until he reaches down and tweaks my distended nub flinging me off the cliff before taking the leap right after me.

Curled up next to him after he undresses us both, cleans me up, then wipes himself down, I murmur as I drift into sleep in his strong arms, "We may face a few uneasy days, but we'll face them together."

He buries his face in my neck. "That we will."

With that assurance, I fall into dreamland knowing my love's safe and sound.

CHAPTER THIRTEEN
PRESENT

Charlie

I'VE BEEN LABELED A SOLDIER, but even soldiers are soft beneath their armor. Mara was one of my soft points. My eyes cast in the direction of the couch, where Rhoswen is comforting members of my family after she let me go a few moments ago.

She's another. I'm not certain if she realizes just how deeply she's buried inside my heart.

Yet.

Does it scare me? Yes. I've survived through too much, almost lost too many people to not be frightened of love. But Rhoswen is different. She appeared, sure. But her presence wasn't a hit and run. It grew roots.

Moving away from the fireplace, I accept the glass of water Jon hands me with gratitude. Sipping it, I wait for the restlessness to settle around the room before sliding Mara back into that place of my heart that will always be reserved for her. When I'm able to speak without choking, I put the glass on the mantle and clap my hands to get everyone's attention. "Alright. That concludes the grief portion of tonight's program."

A few reluctant titters filter through the heaviness of the room. Good. I need my family breathing before I keep going. More comfortable with what I'm about to share, I sit down on the stone hearth. The next part of my marriage journey just requires blunt honesty.

After all, the man who is going to be surprised by most of what I'm about to share, is on the floor with his arm wrapped around his wife. "After Mara, I took a break from marriage."

Mitch's head snaps in my direction immediately. He knows I'm about to start talking about his aunt and has likely been keeping track of the timeline waiting for this very moment. "A long one?" he asks.

"Long enough that I stopped receiving mail order catalogs from jewelry stores suggesting engagement rings," I deadpan.

That earns a real laugh.

"I was alone for years," I continue. "By design. I worked. I slept.

I hunted down missing kids. I didn't ask my heart to do anything ambitious."

Mitch tilts his head. "You were okay with that?"

I shrug. "I was functional. Which, after what I'd lost, felt like winning."

I feel Rhoswen's quiet presence not too far from me. I don't look at her, but I feel her energy flowing through me. Much like the first time I told her, the ghost of her hand glides up and down my back giving me strength.

"Which brings us to wife number four." I say.

"Aunt Rita," Mitch clarifies.

"Take note; she's the longest one. Ten years, give or take. Not including the divorce proceedings."

That sets the room buzzing. I calm the nosy bees down when I talk over them. "I met Rita when I joined Laskey Investigations." Silence falls. "I was hired to lead their Missing Persons and Children Division. It was easy for me to leave the West Coast. New city. New job. New version of me that didn't have memories of uniforms, deployments, or Mara."

"Did she work for Laskey?" Colby asks.

"No, she was the boss's sister—Rita Laskey." Then I add dryly, "Which might be why he canned my ass after the divorce went through."

Mitch snorts. "You're kidding."

"I wish. I was already out the door when I met Caleb and Keene." My brow furrows. "Rita was already in my life socially because of the company—fundraisers, charity events, holiday parties. She was and is smart. Polished. Easy to be around."

"Did you love her?" Mitch wonders.

I don't dodge it. "No, but I respected her."

"That's not the same thing," Mitch says carefully.

"It's not. But after the loss I sustained with Mara, it was safe." I lift my glass from the mantle and take a drink. "Affection wasn't such a bad thing. Rita didn't demand much from me. And at the time, that felt like a mercy."

Mitch frowns. "So you married her because she was...what? Comfortable?"

"I married her because I genuinely cared for her. I wanted stability and I thought love could grow from that," I say. "And because I fully intended to keep my vows."

That lands because Mitch knows how my marriage ended. He winces.

"I took vows with Rita. I knew if I did, they wouldn't be casual or flimsy words. Those words meant everything—particularly after Mara. I truly believed we could have a solid partnership."

"Did she know about Mara?" Mitch asks.

"She knew my heart had been shattered," I replied quietly. "I didn't hide that from her. But we married too quickly for me to work up the courage to be able to discuss the specifics."

Mitch leans forward now. "Okay—but you stayed ten years. Why did you choose then to—"

"Penance," I finish for him. "And I confused my acceptance for the previous sins of my other marriages for what your aunt was doing to me in ours."

He nods slowly. "So when she cheated—"

At his words, the collective inhale should be enough to drain all the oxygen in the room. The only person who doesn't react is Rhoswen. The night I told her, she waited for me to finish before asking me, *"Were you punishing yourself with Rita over Mara's death?"*

Sometimes it's a bitch to be in love with such a smart woman. Shaking myself out of my reverie, I answer Mitch flatly. "I didn't condone her actions. Not at any time."

"But you stayed," he presses. "How does a man with your honor let that happen?"

The question is sharp—but fair. "Because, as it was recently pointed out to me, I may have felt I deserved it."

Mitch tries to speak but can't. The rest of the room is silent as they try to absorb the idea that I knew I was being cheated on and let it happen.

"Straight up, Rita and I never should have gotten married. I was emotionally absent from our marriage from almost day one."

Mitch blinks. "You're saying—"

"I was tied to her by a piece of paper but still in love with another woman," I put it as blunt as possible. "She told me that, and she was right. Sure, I showed up. Paid bills. Fixed things. Asked surface-level questions. But was that enough? No. All I did was abandon my wife with better manners."

That hits him harder than I expect. Mitch starts. "So, when you found out..."

"I wasn't heartbroken," I say flatly.

His brows skyrocket. "Not at all?"

"No. But I was disappointed." Despite how bad of a husband I was, I've attended enough therapy sessions and spoken to Rita enough over the years that I feel my truth has as much validation as hers. I've owned up to my mistakes and she's taken ownership for hers. "I wish she'd come to me first. That she'd looked me in the eye and said 'This isn't working. I need more.' Instead, we both made a mockery of our vows."

Mitch nods slowly. "You would've listened."

"Yes," I say. "Because despite how it might have appeared, I did care for your aunt, Mitch."

"That's...disturbingly comforting."

"Aptly put."

"So why stay after her first affair?" he asks. "Why not walk then?"

"What's the SEAL motto?"

"The only easy day was yesterday."

"Exactly. If it's broke, you don't walk. I didn't bail when things FUBARed. Because a woman I lost taught me taking vows meant you tried. And when I lost her, I realized that meant if I tried again, I'd give it my all—even if it cost me."

I pause, then try to make a joke, "Also, my divorce lawyer threatened to force me to sign a retainer that made the national debt look like chump change."

Mitch snorts. "I don't doubt it."

"When I found out, I confronted Rita before it spread too far in New York social circles. We talked. Like adults. No screaming. No plates thrown."

"She didn't beg?" Mitch asks.

"No," I say. "She was relieved to have the guilt lifted. Sadly, it didn't stop her from doing it again."

That says everything.

"Eventually, we made a mutual decision to end it before resentment turned us into people we didn't want to become. That, of course, didn't stop her brother being a complete douchebag and firing me," I add.

Caleb drawls, "His stupidity was my immense gain," for which a round of applause goes around the room.

Mitch cocks his head to the side. "You both seem... okay now?"

"We're cordial. She's not the villain of my story." I scan the room. "But I don't excuse the choice."

That distinction matters.

"So," I conclude, "that was wife number four. The longest. But I have one thing to say. If you think I regret one minute of that marriage, you all need to have your heads checked. My marrying Rita Laskey gave me the best gift I could ever ask for."

"What's that, Uncle Charlie?" Kalie asks from the back where she's standing with her cousins.

"All of you. I was working for Laskey when your parents came in to ensure their identities couldn't be traced from who they used to be to who they are now. Six young adults who had world-weary eyes and souls that were as bruised as mine." I find Phil's eyes first. Then Cassidy's. Emily's. Ali's. Corinna's. And then I meet the lens of Holly's camera knowing she's staring directly at me.

The room hums—not with shock, but understanding. It's this family's credo—we all bleed a little for love.

I straighten, rolling my shoulders again. "That brings us to wife number five."

The air shifts instantly. I tilt my head, the corner of my mouth curling. "Now that one? That's where everyone knows things got... criminal."

Rhoswen growls deep in her throat and the fierceness of it—like a lioness protecting her pack—grounds me. My focus turns to Cassidy, who I note reaches for Rhoswen's hand and squeezes it, not for her comfort, but to calm my woman down.

That gesture alone makes what I'm about to remind them of no less brutal, but still necessary to explain. For the first time all night, I allow myself a smile that isn't hollow—because surviving my previous marriages taught me one thing.

If you can still love, you're worth someone loving you.

CHAPTER FOURTEEN
PRESENT

Charlie

I DON'T WAIT for the room to reset before I launch into the culmination of my story. "Wife number five is the reason you never met anyone I was involved with until tonight."

There's no room for joking in my voice. There's no humor when we broach how we almost lost Cassidy.

Thinking of this one hurts every time I imagine that viper. Clearing my throat, I mutter, "Vanessa came into my life during my divorce from Rita. It was one of those 'meet cutes' you girls keep waxing on about. She spilled her coffee on me. I told her it was okay. She demanded my number to pay for the clean up. I gave her the business line. She called, asked me to dinner."

"Thought she was good natured. A breath of fresh air. She knew from the beginning I was coming out of a messy divorce. Nothing happened until that was done. Then it was a whirlwind."

Then shame hits when I admit, "She reminded me of Mara. So much, it was like having a second chance."

The room is silent.

"It wasn't her physical looks. But she knew how to play her part in the ways that mattered. Sweetness. Kindness. The way she listened like no one else mattered." I let out a breath through my nose. "I should've known better. But grief—especially the kind you never resolve—rewires your instincts. You lean toward familiar instead of your instincts warning you against the truth."

No one interrupts me.

"Everyone claimed they were happy for me, even if they weren't." I huff out a breath. "I remember Phil mentioning during a quick lunch in the city that it was good to see me smiling again. And I internalized that meant I was finally doing something right."

"By then, Laskey had sold up and I was working full time for Hudson Investigations. I was still keeping track of my kids. Before Caleb even knew Cassidy existed, he passed me in the hall one day. Mentioned I was less grumpy. Still, because of the class of data I had access to, he insisted Vanessa have a background check. It came back clean. No flags."

Caleb's head twists, anger a pulsing tic at his temple. I remind him, "None of us knew how deep the rot went at Hudson."

"This isn't on you, Charlie," he bites out.

"It's not on you either," I retort.

He jerks his chin up in ascent. "What none of us knew was Vanessa was studying me. Mapping me. Using proximity to collect information I didn't even realize I was giving and feeding it to someone who was laying a trap."

I look around the room, meeting eyes one by one. "She was part of the larger scheme to dismantle this family."

A sharp growl comes from somewhere near the couch. Since I'm not looking in that direction, I can only surmise it's Keene recalling what we went through in those few minutes when we almost lost his sister—Caleb's wife.

"She fed what she learned to people who were paying her for the information. One woman in particular who didn't care who was hurt so long as her image was preserved as she eliminated any threats against her."

My hands curl slowly into fists. "And one of those threats was Cassidy."

I recall running into the library, brandishing my weapon on Caleb's mother—shock and horror fighting for equal space until

I shut myself down. Keene falling apart. Blood spilled—Cassidy's blood. The paramedics rushing her out the door.

"Until she woke up, I'm certain none of us slept." I don't dress it up. "I—we—stood watch over her. We memorized exits. I ran scenarios in my head trying to figure out who leaked the information. Then, Caleb called in the Feds."

I swallow hard. "When I was questioned, they made me replay every conversation I'd ever had with Vanessa. Nothing I'd ever mentioned about Cassidy or her family was in the files at Hudson, but it was enough for the inside analysts to start digging without triggering any alarms. Essentially, I'd handed over my family on a silver platter because I refused to admit I wasn't still broken from something that happened a decade and a half earlier."

My voice hardens. "When the Feds took her away, I stood there and wished—just once—I could play judge and jury instead of handing her over for questioning."

Everyone, either through living it or hearing it from their family, knows exactly what kind of rage I'm feeling. "She was charged. Convicted. Accessory to attempted murder." I give a short, humorless laugh. "And it wasn't enough. Because no conviction changes the fact that Cassidy almost died. No sentence erased the fact that I was the door Vanessa walked through to get close enough."

Understanding starts to settle in when I say bluntly, "For a long time, I didn't trust myself. Not my instincts, not my judgement.

Not the ability to tell the difference between kindness and manipulation."

I gesture vaguely at the entire room. "And I wasn't willing to gamble with your lives again just because I was lonely."

The women's eyes fill with tears but I can't let it affect me. I reach for my water and swallow a few gulps. Once I'm certain my voice is steady, I continue, "So I stopped dating. I stopped letting anyone get close enough to matter. I built a perimeter around all of us."

By now, even the men's eyes are damp. Caleb's scrubbing his forearm against his cheek even before I say, "I chose isolation because it was safer than risking you. I lived with that choice willingly."

Then my head turns and I meet Rhoswen's dark eyes head on. "Then, I took my vacation, which included a bus tour in Scotland. There was this stranger—a pretty American— chastising the tour guide for giving out inaccurate information. She called him out in front of every passenger for his inaccuracy of the fall of the MacDonald clan to the Campbells. I used my multi-tool to dig up a rock for her to keep as a keepsake from where her people slaughtered my ancestors. It was forty degrees, and my hands froze, but she wanted it. So I did it."

Rhoswen's lips curve in remembrance. "It sits proudly next to my stuffed Highland Cow."

I roll my eyes at her before turning my eyes back toward the rest of the family. "I'm not sorry for wanting you all to meet Rhoswen. But there are two things I will apologize for."

"What could you possibly want to apologize for?" Corinna asks from the shelter of Colby's arms.

"I'm sorry for not sharing all of this with you before now." Then my gaze drifts over to Rhoswen. "And I'm sorry for not introducing you to Rhoswen sooner. I should have trusted my family."

Cassidy pushes up from her seat. She makes a beeline directly for me. Before I can stop her, she throws her arms around my waist—tiny thing that she is. Soon after, I feel the arms of the rest of my "kids"—Phil, Emily, Alison, Corinna, and Holly— around me as well.

Overlapping each other, their voices finally make me believe I'm worth the vow tattooed on my forearm.

"We love you, Charlie."

"You saved us."

"You didn't set anything in motion."

"You helped stop it."

I don't argue. I've said what needed saying to all the people who matter the most—my family and Rhoswen. The people I expect to be in my life for a long time. After a long moment, I decide I've done enough talking. Because tonight isn't about any more epiphanies. It's about family.

Joy.

Revelry.

And we're well past time showing Rhoswen we excel at celebrating that.

CHAPTER FIFTEEN
SIX DAYS AGO

Rhoswen

MORNINGS WITH CHARLIE can be dangerous. After a night of pleasure, I wake in a malleable daze. Nothing exists beyond the sheets that are warmed by his body.

It's a daily injection of hope that I want to last every single day of the year.

We didn't go out last night, electing for our own private celebration. Knowing I spend my days with students, we elected to welcome the new year barefoot in his kitchen, slow dancing to music and sipping wine from the same spot in the same glass.

He kissed me at midnight like our hearts are in their own gravitation pull.

Now, I'm still up in the memories. Not in a hurry to move but knowing I'll need to soon.

I'm sprawled across Charlie's stomach. His muscular arm holds me tight against the side of his body—keeping me close not just in body but in spirit. I trace the faint scar near his collarbone with my lips. He exhales, fingers tightening slightly at my hip.

"You're awake," he murmurs.

"Mm. Have been."

"How long?"

"Long enough to validate that when you drink red wine, you snore very lightly."

He scoffs. "I do not."

"No, you're right. You conduct a marching band of elephants out of your mouth when you snore."

His chest rumbles beneath my cheek. "That's...specific."

I smile against his skin. "You want specific? You should read the paper I graded last week on the historical context of elephants during the Renaissance."

His hand drifts up my back, slow and absentmindedly. I revel in it like a cat lounging lazily in the sun. I could stay like this all day. Which is probably why the Gods choose this moment for him to open his mouth and say my name in a way that makes me instantly wary. "Rhoswen."

Lifting my head, I prop my chin on a fist I make on his chest. His eyes are soft, lips pursed. His face is thoughtful in a way that means he's been turning something over in his mind. "Yes?"

"There's something I want to ask you."

There it is. My stomach tightens—not painfully, just enough to register that this matters. "Are we going on an adventure? Were your elephant noises a clue?" I tease.

"Not quite, but not entirely wrong." He doesn't rush. Charlie never rushes important things. He slides his thumb along my chin, grounding himself as much as me. "You've heard me talk about my extended family."

"The Freemans, Lockwoods, Marshalls..." I'm about to spout off every branch when he lays a finger against my lips.

"You got it. We have some unusual traditions. As the family's grown—people celebrating holidays with extended relatives— the family decided not too long ago to celebrate Twelfth Night together."

I blink. "Really?"

"Yes."

"Like... the Shakespeare play? Costumes and chaos?"

A corner of his mouth twitches. "The chaos is a certainty. As for the rest, you'll appreciate it. More like the old tradition of one last gathering before the grateful return to real life."

"That sounds...enthusiastic and terrifying."

He chuckles. "Two very valid words for it." He shifts slightly so we're more face to face, the blanket slipping down to our waists. His gaze doesn't leave mine. "I want you to come with me."

The words land softly but the shot to my heart is anything but that. I can't speak, not because I don't want to shout "Yes!" at the top of my lungs but because if I try to open my mouth to speak, I'm going to curl into a ball and sob at the implication of his invitation.

Charlie wants me to meet his family. The people he's talked about from the day we met—first in fragments and anecdotes then with full stories and recriminations. These are the people who pulled him from the depths of his despair without realizing they made him into the man I fell in love with. They have only the scarcest idea of his history but he's saved them from theirs.

They're the men and women who will meet me and decide whether or not I'm good enough for the man I've already vowed to love forever. My heart thumps so hard against my ribs, I'm certain he must feel it. "I—" I stutter. "Are you sure?"

His voice is completely certain. "Yes. I wouldn't ask if I wasn't."

Meeting family has never been easy for me. Even before I became a professor, I was terrified of parent-teacher conferences. I'm an excellent educator. Give me a lecture hall full of skeptical undergrad students and I'll hold my own without breaking a sweat.

But a living room full of people who love the man I love?

Can I ask for tequila this early in the new year?

"What does their Twelfth Night look like?" I ask, curious in addition to buying myself a moment to regulate my heart rate.

"Too much food. Too many opinions. Kids running underfoot. Dancing on tables. The usual."

"Dancing on tables. You?" I tease weakly.

"Not a chance in hell. Usually the women. Well, and Phil," he corrects himself.

I laugh, then stop as the nerves creep back in.

"And they'll be okay...with me?" I ask quietly.

His thumb brushes my cheek. "Rhoswen."

I meet his eyes.

"These are the people who made me want to stay when I wasn't certain anything could. I've watched them learn to dream, panic and run. Breathe when there was barely any hope, believe in nothing, and walk through fire." His voice lowers. "I want them to meet the woman who convinced me I could do the same."

The weight of his words steals my breath. "Don't say that if you don't mean it."

"That's exactly why you need to hear me say it to you. And they need to know I mean it."

I sit up slightly, wrapping the blanket around myself as if to ward off any negative emotions. "What if they don't like me?"

He smiles gently. "They will."

"You don't know that."

"I do," he says.

"How?" I demand.

"Because you're honest and you love me. In our family those are the only two pieces of currency that matter."

I hesitate. "And if I mess up?"

"Then you'll fit right in." He thinks about it for a second. "Especially your cow obsession. Pretty certain Kalie wanted to bring back half of Banff on her uncle's plane the last time she was there."

Even as I straighten up to whack Charlie with my pillow, hope, terror and excitement tangle together inside of me. I blurt out, "Why now?"

"Because it's time, Rhoswen. It's time to take the next step," he finishes.

Charlie's answer robs me of speech. So I nod.

Slowly. Deliberately.

Finally, when I regain the power, I give him the answer he's hoping for. "Yes."

His exhale is immediate. Relieved. Like he'd been bracing without realizing it. He confirms, "Yes to Twelfth Night?"

"Yes," I repeat. "I'll go."

He pulls me into his chest, holding me tightly—not like he's afraid I'll disappear, but like he's grateful I didn't.

I rest my cheek against his heart again, listening to its steady rhythm.

"I'm going to panic," I warn.

"I'll be right here."

"I might say something boring at the wrong time."

"They'll survive."

"I might need to escape."

"I'll hold the door to the escape hatch."

I smile, then grow serious. "Thank you. For trusting me with that part of you."

His lips brush my hair. "Thank you for wanting it."

We lie together entangled for a while longer each of us thinking about Twelfth Night and the possibilities of it. For the first time in a long time, the thought of stepping into someone else's world doesn't feel like a risk.

It feels like an invitation.

Wrapped in Charlie's arms, I let myself believe that maybe—just maybe—they'll accept I belong there too.

CHAPTER SIXTEEN
PRESENT

Charlie

THE NIGHT AIR is crisp enough to erase the reminders of the past. Standing behind the farm, I can hear the muffled and distant noise of my family. I inhale, slow and deep, and let the cold air clean my soul out.

I told Rhoswen I needed a few minutes. She didn't pepper me with questions or concerns that would've felt like additional pressure. She just stood there in the middle of the great room while the family buzzed behind her. Incredibly, she looked at me the exact same way she did before we ever walked through the door for Twelfth Night.

Then she rose onto her toes, kissed me, and said, "Okay. Take all the time that you need."

Just that simple. Just that easy.

Then she stepped back to let me regroup because she knows after the emotional reckoning I just put myself through, I need time to ground myself back in the now.

Above me, the heavens don't care how many times I've been married. They don't care about graves or betrayals or courtrooms or the week I didn't sleep because if I closed my eyes, all my mind conjured up was Cassidy's last breath. Then gasping for air when I jolted awake imagining someone was waking me to tell me it was true.

I stand there, hands shoved in my pockets, shoulders hunched slightly against the wind, and let my thoughts drift to the woman I left inside with my family.

Rhoswen.

I brought her here and assured her of her welcome. Instead, she was my rock as I was the one put on the hot seat. Confessing all the parts of me I'd tucked behind the mask I wear around my family. Never to be revealed during family time. For longer than I can remember, I've been 'Uncle' Charlie. The man who protects, the man who laughs.

Not the man who demolishes Twelfth Night with my past.

But, as my glorious historian tells me, history repeats itself and we have to learn from it. *I wonder what my family feels about what they learned tonight.* I scuff the snow covered ground with the toe of my boot.

That's when I hear the hiss. It's the only indication the back slider has been opened. It's faint, but it carries in the cold like a whisper.

I don't turn. I don't have to.

Footsteps follow—steady, careful, like whoever it is doesn't want to startle me. The crunch of snow is familiar. The weight distribution. The hesitation on the second step. The small pause like they're deciding how to approach a man who just laid himself bare.

I know exactly who it is without turning around.

Keene.

He stops a few feet behind me. Close enough to be present. Far enough to give me space. The wind shifts. I catch a hint of bourbon and woodsmoke. He clears his throat like he doesn't want to interrupt some deep introspective. "Charlie," he says.

I keep my gaze on the stars. "If you're here to tell me I should've kept my mouth shut, you're too late. I've lectured myself three times since I walked out the back door."

A beat.

Then Keene—Keene, who usually has a smirk welded to his face—declares, "I'm here to tell you I was an ass."

I blink once to make certain I'm awake. The words make sense, but not coming from this man. "That's one way to put it."

He huffs a quiet laugh, but it's not his usual cocky one. There's a rough edge to it, like he's scraping the words out of himself. "I was a dick because...I don't know. Because for so long, you've been this father figure in my life. It wasn't easy to realize your life was changing and I wasn't there for you."

I turn my head slightly—not all the way, but enough to catch him in my peripheral. He's standing with his hands shoved into his jacket pockets, shoulders hunched, face flushed from cold and guilt. It doesn't look good on him. "I wanted to make certain she was good enough for you," he states, then shakes his head. "That doesn't sound right when I say it out loud."

"It doesn't, but I know what you mean."

"I mean, it's not like you haven't had any women since your last marriage."

"Wow, Keene. I didn't know you were so interested in my love life. If I didn't know you had Ali, I'd almost think you had a crush on me."

"Don't flatter yourself."

Ahh, there's the Keene I know and love. I deadpan, "Impossible when you do it so well."

He snorts, the sound escaping before he can stop it. Then his expression sobers again, and the smirk fades like someone wiped it away. "I really do apologize, Charlie. I was an ass at dinner."

I face forward again, eyes back on the sky. It's easier to keep him on the hook if I'm not looking at his face. "I expected it," I say. "So did Rhoswen."

I feel his curiosity pulsate through the air. "Really?"

I hum in ascent. Then I let out the real reason I had to escape. "What I didn't expect was to validate who we are to each other by dragging everyone through my past."

Keene is quiet, absorbing my words. The house behind us is illuminated with life—laughter, shouts, singing. *Oh, god. I hope Jake keeps Emily away from the karaoke machine.* My stomach pitches and rolls at the thought of that topping off the evening.

Then Keene vocalizes what he's thinking, "I don't think you ruined anything."

I glance at him again. His lips are in a firm line, eyes steady on mine.

"I just made half the room cry."

"Yeah," he replies. "Because they love you, you stubborn bastard."

A choked laugh escapes before I can stop it. It comes out rougher than I mean it to.

Keene continues, voice lower now. Words careful. "I think you just gave us more to celebrate about who we are—how we became this family."

I still. It's such an unexpected sentence from him that it takes a second to land. "What do you mean?"

"Amaryllis. Alteo. Our women wear the mark symbolizing pride, determination, and beauty. The men, the arrow that pierced Amaryllis's heart to make her bleed while falling in love. You? You're the original person who wears both marks. Isn't that what tonight's really all about?"

My throat tightens as Keene's words penetrate. He continues. "When we decided to celebrate Twelfth Night, we came together. We ate and drank. But did we ever stop to celebrate the reason we even have this. The reason we're together at all?"

I can't do anything but stare at him. My earliest memories of Keene aren't of the man he grew into but as the sanctimonious prick who was searching for his long lost sister. He used his vicious tongue as a sword to wield off any more emotions to cause him pain.

Until this family rescued him as much as it did me.

"You saved them long before you found a way to keep the rest of us steady." Keene swallows. "When things got ugly. When..." He trails off, then shakes his head like he's refusing to name old wounds. "You've been by our sides. Every time."

My throat tightens. I look away quickly, back to the stars. "Keene, there's no need for this."

"Don't. Please." He steps closer, just one pace, so he's beside me now instead of behind me. He doesn't crowd. Just aligns.

"The stories you told tonight?" he continues. "They weren't just about wives. They weren't just about you getting screwed over or making bad calls or being too damn honorable for your own good."

"Too damn stubborn," I correct automatically.

Keene's mouth twitches. "That too." His chin jerks in the direction of the house. "They were the groundwork for how we live the way we do, love the way we can. Why we found our families and not once had to let them go."

I swallow hard.

"You didn't ruin anything, Charlie." Keene says. "You reminded us what we're celebrating."

I stare at him before swallowing down my tears. Then I ask him, "Did you practice that on your way out here?"

He growls, "Shut up."

I laugh quietly. The routine of Keene being, well, Keene eases something in my chest. "You're impossible. But I love you too."

He snorts, then sobers again. "You didn't have to tell us all that."

"I know."

"But you did to shield Rhoswen."

"Yeah," I admit quietly.

Keene's gaze flicks toward the house. "She's in there with the family instead of out here with you."

It's not a question. Keene's perceptive when he bothers to be. "You knew we'd accept her."

"Because I love her." There. The words are out there.

He's silent for a beat. Then, "You told her first."

Again—statement, not question.

My chest tightens. "Yeah."

"So... she's the real deal?"

I huff. "What, you thought I rented her?"

"Honestly, Charlie? Do you want me to answer that?"

I glare at him. "Boy, you're lucky I'm emotionally fragile right now or I'd kick your ass."

"You're never that emotionally fragile," he says, then immediately winces. "Okay, that sounded—"

"I know what you meant," I cut in.

Then he clears his throat and does something I don't expect.

He nudges my shoulder. Lightly. Almost like a son to his father. "Come back inside."

I stare at the stars a second longer. "In a minute."

Keene doesn't push. He just stands there with me, silent. After a beat, he says quietly, "For what it's worth... I'm glad you told us."

I don't trust my voice, so I nod once.

Keene nods back like we've made some silent agreement. Then he turns toward the house, pauses at the corner, and calls my name.

I turn around and find his trademark smirk—worn like armor again, but softer now, less sharp—back in place. "If you tell anyone I said any of that. I'll deny it and claim you hallucinated due to Emily singing karaoke."

I manage a real smile. "If Emily's singing karaoke, there's no way in hell I'm coming back inside."

He snorts. "Get inside, Charlie. Before Cass and Ali hand her the mic."

After he disappears, I stay for a moment longer and let the cold sting my cheeks letting Keene's words penetrate.

Maybe he's right. This family isn't built on perfection. I've known that from the beginning. It's built on truth and survival and choosing each other anyway.

And they chose me.

Rhoswen chose me.

Both feel incredible.

I exhale, then turn toward the house. Toward warmth. Toward laughter.

And the woman who kissed me and told me to take all the time I needed—and meant it.

CHAPTER SEVENTEEN
PRESENT

Rhoswen

THE HOUSE DOESN'T quiet when Charlie steps outside.

The moment the door closes behind him, the energy in the room shifts—subtle at first, then unmistakable. Chairs scrape. Glasses clink. Then laughter builds, slowly but surely.

Music starts playing but still, I feel it before I see them. I take a sip of my drink from a woman who introduced herself as Jilly handed to me, buying myself a second.

Or so I thought.

The oldest Freemans descend on me. All of them wearing expressions that range between unholy to delighted to determined. Judging by the gleam in their eyes, I'm fairly certain they already like me.

Which might be worse.

"So," Emily smiles like she's asking about the weather, "what size dress do you wear?"

I choke. Just a little. "I—what?"

Alison jumps in. "And what style do you like the best?"

Corinna tilts her head. "We keep a lot in stock since sample sizes are cruel."

Phil grins like he knows exactly what's happening—adds, "We just like to be prepared."

"Prepared. For what, exactly? A natural disaster? A heist? A hostile takeover?"

They all burst into laughter. Cassidy reaches out and squeezes my arm. "They have a lot less chaos, unfortunately."

"Are there wrong answers? Am I being graded?"

"Oh no," Emily says breezily. "This is just curiosity."

"Purely academic," Alison adds.

"Academic my ass," Holly yells from the kitchen.

I glance over and spot her perched on the kitchen counter, camera already in hand, lens trained directly on me. She grins when she catches my eye. "Don't mind me," she says. "I'm just documenting... whatever this is."

My pulse picks up. "Okay," I say slowly, setting my empty glass down. "Why are you asking about my dress size?"

They exchange looks. Quick. Loaded.

"Well," Jilly says breezily. Married to Holly's husband's boss, she's a close friend of the family. After handing me a refilled drink, she says, "You never know."

"Know what?"

"When things are needed," another voice intrudes.

Unfortunately, I'd just taken a sip when I realize who spoke. Choking, I manage, "Oh, god. You're Kee Long."

"Call me Kelsey. It's my real name," my literary idol replies as she whacks me on the back.

"Right," I manage faintly, praying I don't pass out before Charlie gets back. Then I shake some sense into myself. "Wait. What things?"

"Rhoswen, just trust us." Phil says gently, as if addressing a skittish animal. "By the way, what are your favorite flowers?"

I stare at him like he might be a rabid Highland cow—unpredictable but still adorable. "Sunflowers and peonies."

A flash goes off. Holly announces, "Got a great one. Totally Christmas worthy for next year."

"Christmas? Next year?" *Did we just skip three hundred and fifty-ish days in an unexplained time warp?*

I must have spoke aloud because Phil claps his hands, delighted. "Rhoswen, that's epic. A time warp."

The sisters talk over each other so fast I'm not certain at this point if they slipped something into my drink or if I'm seriously hallucinating. "I told you she was smart!"

"She's a professor, of course she got it."

"Oh, I *knew* she was the one."

My heart starts to pound—not in panic, exactly, but in terror. "You're planning my *wedding?*"

"Not planning," Cassidy corrects. "Discussing."

"Pre-planning," says Alison.

"Light scheming," Phil offers.

I press a hand to my chest. "You cannot do that. You absolutely cannot do that."

"Why not?" someone asks, genuinely confused.

"Because—because I don't even know if Charlie wants that."

All the commotion in the room stills. Five feminine eyes soften. Phil's grin fades into something thoughtful. "Well," Corinna says carefully, "he brought you here."

"I know. And I don't take that lightly. I just—" I take in a deep breath to give credence to my next words. "I love him. Truly. If marriage is something he wants someday, I'd say yes. I'll scream my answer. But if it's not... that's okay too."

They listen. Really listen.

"I'm not here to steer him away from who he is, from the man he's worked so hard to become," I continue. "I'm here because I choose him."

The quiet that follows isn't awkward. It's awed. Finally, it's Phil who breaks the silence. "That is the perfect answer to all our questions."

Corinna steps forward and squeezes my hand. "You're already one of us, you know."

Emily nods, curls bobbing. "Charlie doesn't bring people here unless they matter."

Alison smiles through suspiciously shiny eyes. "And anyone who loves him the way you just described... well. We protect our own."

My throat tightens unexpectedly. "I didn't expect this kind of acceptance."

Holly finally hops down from her perch, camera bobbing around her neck. "Nobody ever does," she says cheerfully. "That's how we get you."

I laugh, swiping beneath my eyes. "You're all... a lot."

"Thank you," several voices say in unison.

Cassidy pulls me into a hug. Then more and more arms wrap around us. They're warm and overwhelming in the best possible way. I'm mid-laugh, mid-hug, mid-*how did this happen*, when I feel him.

Charlie's presence registers before I can unearth myself from the group hug to get to him. Then I feel his warmth press into my back, solid and familiar, and I exhale without realizing I was holding my breath.

His mouth brushes my ear, low and amused. "Not now, but who knows what the future holds."

I lean back into him. "You shouldn't feel pressured."

He spins me around. "Never from you, Rhoswen."

Deciding to lighten the mood a bit, I tease, "Besides, if all family events are like this, it might take me a few decades to accept."

His body vibrates with laughter. "Actually, they're normally worse."

I tilt my head up, incredulous. "You lie."

Just then, the music cranks up—loud, joyful, unmistakably *danceable*. Charlie's arms tighten around me as the room explodes into motion. Someone whoops. Someone else claps. Two of the younger women immediately start claiming end tables. Faintly, I ask, "Did I hear that correctly?"

"Yes."

"You weren't lying."

"No, I wasn't."

A woman with shiny black hair hops onto the table. Another kicks off her shoes. A gorgeous man who has Corinna's eyes grabs a bottle and raises it like a trophy.

I stare, astounded before bursting out laughing.

Charlie presses a kiss to my temple. "Welcome to the family, Professor."

I look around—at the chaos, the laughter, the warmth—and something settles deep in my chest.

Happiness that all these years, Charlie had this. That he invited me to share it with him tonight.

As the music swells and the room fills with movement and joy I expected at a Twelfth Night celebration, I don't hesitate to join in.

After all, they're Charlie's family.

EPILOGUE
SIX MONTHS LATER

Rhoswen

THE SCENT OF LAVENDER, peonies, and sunflowers drift through the air, carried on a breeze warm enough to kiss my bare shoulders. Rows of chairs are filled with familiar faces—some laughing, some wiping their eyes already, some doing both at once. Sunlight filters through the oak trees that ring the lawn behind the building where I first had dinner on Twelfth Night.

Holly was right.

Garden wedding.

Emily designed my dress—an original tea-length dress that has a whole new plaid that combines both the tartans of mine and Charlie's clans bound together with arrows and amaryllises. My hair is half up, caught at the side with white pearl clips borrowed from Cassidy.

I catch a glimpse of myself reflected in the window as I step into position, and for a moment I barely recognize the woman looking back.

Standing here, barefoot in the grass, dress brushing my calves, I realize peace has been something Charlie and I have chosen every single day with each other, for each other, since he unburdened himself.

That's why I chose to walk down the aisle on my own. Even though almost everyone offered, it was important to me. It is my walk, my choice, my gift to present myself to the man I love. We are choosing to move forward together, step by deliberate step, heart steady, head high.

Together.

At the end of the aisle, waiting for me, is Charlie. I take the first step toward him. Then another. And I keep going until my heart is ready to burst.

Sure, we're older. We both have a few more lines at the corner of our eyes than the average bride and groom, which we both attribute to more smiles and laughter. He claims he has a touch more silver in his beard than when we first started dating. But he's still the same grounded presence that sat next to me on a tour bus and listened to me rant over the inaccuracies being spoken by our tour bus driver.

When his eyes meet mine, the world narrows in that familiar way it always does with him. The rest of the world fades into background noise.

Keene stands behind him waiting to perform our ceremony, which still boggles my mind. Who knew Keene was such a sentimentalist beneath all the pompousness? Well, I guess his sister, wife, daughters, and Charlie. Still, I'm in awe when the man who can't help but take potshots at his brother-in-law clears his throat and looks out at the gathered crowd.

"Normally," Keene begins, "It's Charlie who stands here. He's the one to offer words of wisdom. Words that come from the heart."

A few people laugh softly. Charlie rolls his eyes in a way that makes my chest warm.

"Today," Keene continues, "I want to say this. Had it not been for his wisdom in the days leading up to those weddings, I'm uncertain if any of us would be here today."

The air shifts. This isn't a performance. Keene's about to knock down bodies with his words.

Keene looks back at us. "Charlie has spent his life showing up for people. Sometimes when they deserved it. Often when they didn't. More than once, when it cost him dearly."

My throat tightens. I swallow hard to keep my tears at bay.

"But what he learned—and what he taught the rest of us—is that survival isn't the same as living; the same as loving," Keene says. "He reminded all of us here to fight for that love. Because real love is a choice. Every single day."

Keene looks at me then, and for the first time ever, there's no smirk. "Rhoswen didn't come into Charlie's life to change the man he was. She didn't come to soften him or make him someone else."

I feel every eye on me, but I don't shrink from it.

Keene continues, "She came to stand beside him. To choose him exactly as he is. In doing that, we were all reminded of what falling in love looks like."

Charlie squeezes my fingers tightly, letting me know how much these words affect him.

Keene exhales, then shakes his head slightly. "Which is wild, because if you'd told me six months ago that I'd be officiating this wedding, I would've laughed you out of the room."

That generates a ripple of laughter from the assembled crowd, easing everyone's emotions just a bit.

"But in this case, love found itself on a tour bus. For those of you still waiting, remember, love doesn't always arrive when you're ready for it. Sometimes it shows up when you're least expecting it. And sometimes it arrives when there's a 'hairy coo' vying for your attention."

I'm doing my damndest not to ruin my makeup by crying. I wonder if Alison will mind if I sob all over her husband later. Charlie's hands tighten against mine—grounding me just in time for us to speak our vows.

We make promises grounded in reality, not fantasy. Charlie's voice is steady but the tremble of his hands gives him away. I love him more for that than I ever could for perfection.

When it's my turn, I don't recite anything memorized. I look at him and speak from my heart. "I choose you, in our quiet mornings. In our family's loud chaos. In moments where our pasts overwhelm us and if we ever fear an uncertain future. I choose you—Charles Henderson—not because I want to change a thing about your past, but because I want the man you are for our future."

He swallows hard, eyes bright.

Keene clears his throat again, suspiciously emotional. "By the power vested in me by this family, this garden, and the undeniable fact you both went to Town Hall to make this official two days ago, it gives me great pleasure to pronounce you both emotionally married. Charlie, you once said this to me and Ali— you may now kiss your bride."

The cheer that goes up is loud and unrestrained and utterly perfect. Charlie kisses me like he's been waiting forever for Keene to announce it. Maybe he has. Maybe this union is special because one of his 'kids' performed the ceremony.

Later—after the applause, after the hugs, after Holly inevitably corners us for photos and whispers "Told you so," we slip away for a moment, just the two of us.

The garden hums with celebration behind us. Laughter rises and falls like a tide. Charlie takes my hands in his, thumbs brushing over my rings like he's grounding himself again.

"How are you feeling?" he asks quietly.

I smile up at him. "Like I can conquer the world."

His mouth curves—not in humor, but in something deeper. Something earned.

We stand there for a moment, the past not forgotten but learned from. The future is ours to make—not perfect, not guaranteed, but real.

That was the vow Charlie made me when he slid my engagement ring on my finger. It's the one I'm going to hold him to.

Forever.

WHERE TO GET HELP

I WANT to start off by reminding people healing is a journey and no two people ever will be exactly at the same location.

Some think there are hard and fast rules that apply to a healing journey—milestones you should hit within a certain time box. Others believe a person should take a break—wait a month for every year you were with a person. Some think it's better to get beneath a new person to get over someone else. I've personally followed the healing journey of a woman who fell in love at fourteen, married at twenty, was together with them before they passed far too early at sixty-four. She is now eighty and has never fallen out of love.

Are any of these responses wrong? Maybe not. However, the important thing to remember is that healing from the devastation of love is as unique as the individual itself. A person should not be told they are "taking too long to heal" nor should they be told they are "healing wrong."

Heal the way you need to.

Psychology Today (link: https://www.psychologytoday.com/us/basics/relationships) reminds everyone to start with open and honest communication with yourself. Devote time and attention to you before devoting time to a new relationship. Don't try to build a new relationship on a fractured foundation. Heal yourself first so you are stronger and can make better choices the second—or, in Charlie's case, the sixth—time around.

Every relationship changes who we are. We can't factory reset to who we were before those interactions, those hurts. Even if we wanted to, it's just not possible.

We need to love ourselves for the person we are now. Then, if you're ready, take that leap of faith toward love.

BONUS SCENE

Rhoswen has a special wedding gift she wants to give Charlie.
Want to find out what it is?

Click below to request the
bonus scene to Free to Vow:

https://dl.bookfunnel.com/hppk5o6w9t

You'll need to sign up to get it delivered directly to your device.
But don't worry! Current subscribers aren't subscribed twice.
Our mailing list tech has your back.

NEWSLETTER

Sign up for my newsletter at https://www.traceyjerald.com/ to get an exclusive prequel to the Amaryllis Series—Phil's Story—as well as access to exclusive bonus scenes after new books release.

ACKNOWLEDGMENTS

To my husband, Nathan, thank you for encouraging my obsession with Highland cows to the point I needed to include them in this story. Also, I will always love you.

To my son, I love you most.

Mom, thank you for always encouraging me to see the world. I love you so much.

My Jen and my Meows, thank you for continuously being part of the Amaryllis magic. I love you all.

To my editing team, The Dynamic Duo, it was a crazy time. Thank you both so much!

To AmyLynn Rhodes, Kristin Lira, and Dawn Hurst, thank you for being the amazing team you are.

For my incredible content team, I'm overwhelmed by your love and support. THANK YOU! MUAH!

To all of the readers who take the time to read my books, thank you for loving Amaryllis from the first day it launched. I am grateful for your continuous support.

XOXO

ABOUT THE AUTHOR

It began when Tracey made up stories in her head as she biked around her neighborhood in Connecticut. Writing, always a passion, interfered with her life when she started rewrote the ends of books instead of finishing college assignments. After all, what was more important, a happily ever after or Greek mythology?

Eventually, she realized the answer was both when she wrote the Amaryllis Series.

Tracey's collection of contemporary romance and women's fiction is available on Amazon.com and free on kindleunlimited. This includes her best-selling Amaryllis Series, Midas Series and Glacier Adventure Series. She has thirty books in print and has participated in several anthologies for reader pleasure as well as charity.

Tracey is dedicated to her own happily ever after, having been married since 2007. She and her husband have one son who is as addicted to his Fortnite as his mama is to coffee.

When she's not busy with her family or writing, Tracey can be found in her home in north Florida plotting her next story, training for a runDisney event, and feeding her addiction to HGTV.